MIXED DOUBLES

Meredith Kingston

Cynthia and Russ were powerful opponents on the tennis courts and good friends – but only that; she was already married and he was engaged. Now, with her marriage ended, Cynthia heads for Russ's Arizona tennis ranch to help her asthma – only to find that Russ had not gotten married. The old friendship bursts into romantic flame under the hot sun. Yet they are so different, and the shadow of their past disillusionment still hung over them. Could they escape from it and find a second chance at love?

SECOND CHANCE AT LOVE
novels in Large Print

ALOHA, YESTERDAY
BELOVED PIRATE
LED INTO SUNLIGHT
MEETING WITH THE PAST
RETURN ENGAGEMENT
SWEET VICTORY
SURPRISE ENDING
THE STEELE HEART
TOO NEAR THE SUN
TENDER TRIUMPH
WINDS OF MORNING

MEREDITH KINGSTON

Mixed Doubles

John Curley & Associates, Inc.
South Yarmouth, Ma.

Library of Congress Cataloging in Publication Data

Kingston, Meredith.
  Mixed doubles.

  Published in large print.
  Originally published: New York : Berkley/ Jove Pub. Group, 1982.
  "Second chance at love."
  1. Large type books.   I. Title.
[PS3561.I53M5   1983]   813'.54   82-23607
ISBN 0–89340–565–5

Meredith Kingston
SECOND CHANCE AT LOVE Books, published by
Berkley/Jove Publishing Group
Copyright © 1982 by Meredith Kingston

Published in Large Print by arrangement with Jove
Publications, Inc.

Distributed in the U.K. and Commonwealth by Magna
Print Books.

Printed in Great Britain

MIXED DOUBLES

2191549

Chapter One

Cynthia wriggled out of her red turtleneck sweater and smoothed her dark brown hair, which she decided had probably lost all its curl during the long day of travel. With a happy sigh, she tossed the sweater on the bed beside her tweed jumper, exulting in the warm Arizona weather that made such clothing out of place. After a quick bath she would change into something appropriate for the casual atmosphere of the Haven Hills Tennis Ranch, and then she would visit her hosts, the Fieldings.

She wondered if Russ and Helene Fielding had changed in the five years since she'd last seen them. They'd all met in college as seniors at Denver University, full of confident dreams for the future. Cynthia and Chuck, already married for a year at that time, had ambitious plans for careers in business. Russ and Helene, engaged to be married right after graduation, wanted to build a guest ranch on a small corner of her father's property in Tucson. They

1

loved to play tennis and enjoyed parties and people, so it seemed to Cynthia that they had set up an ideal goal for their lives together.

Just as she was about to step into the tub, Cynthia heard a light tap on the door and hastily pulled on a robe. Before she could answer it, the door opened and a beautiful young dark-haired woman holding a stack of clean white towels came in.

'Oh, I'm sorry. I didn't know you had checked in already," she said, starting to back out the door, her passkey still in her hand.

"I just arrived in that jazzy red station wagon that picks up your guests at the airport," Cnythia said. "Come on in."

"I'm Merry Spring," the young woman replied shyly as she came into the room. "If there's anything you want while you're here, just ask me."

"That's very nice of you," Cynthia said as she observed the woman with interest. "Pardon me, but you look like you might be of Indian descent. Have I guessed right?"

Merry Spring turned to face Cynthia proudly, seeming to grow an inch or two taller as she straightened up and

2

proclaimed, "I'm a White Mountain Apache, full-blooded."

"How wonderful!" Cynthia exclaimed, pulling the robe more tightly around her slim body and sitting down on the edge of the bed. "My first day here and I meet a real native! Tell me about your tribe. I'd love to learn all about it."

"I grew up at the Fort Apache Indian Reservation, not far from here. It's a tourist area now. We've built new lakes and fishing areas and have campsites and motels."

"That sounds terrific," Cynthia said. She greatly admired people who worked hard to better themselves.

"If you like, someday I'll take you to the Apache Cultural Centre and teach you something about our heritage," Merry Spring offered.

"I'd like that. Oh, I'd better check the water in the tub before it overflows! Excuse me, Merry," Cynthia called as she hurried into the bathroom. "Wait for me if you can. I'll make this a quick dunk."

"I'd better get back to my work," Merry replied as she began fussing over the already spotless room.

The warm water in the tub felt soothing,

3

and Cynthia leaned back and happily considered how lucky she'd been to have a place like this in Tucson to come to. Toward the end of the summer she'd written to the Haven Hills Tenis Ranch, explaining to her old college friends that her bronchial asthma had been severely aggravated by living in the Midwest and that her doctor had advised her to leave before the winter if at all possible. Only a few days later her letter had come back to her by return mail with a message scrawled across the bottom in bold felt pen: "You and Chuck are welcome to stay at this humble hacienda for as long as you want." Russ had filled the rest of the page with a barely legible initial "R."

Cynthia couldn't understand why Russ thought Chuck was coming, too. Maybe he was hinting that he'd like to bring about some sort of reconciliation. She was sure Helene must have told him that she and Chuck had gotten a divorce. Cynthia had written to Helene several times since leaving college and had explained in the note on her last Christmas card that she and Chuck had finally admitted that their differences had become what is politely referred to in divorce courtrooms as

4

"irreconcilable."

Yes, that was a descriptive enough word. Cynthia had finally reached a point where she couldn't reconcile herself to the hostile dinner-table conversations, to Chuck bragging about his latest victory in the office intrigues he enjoyed so much. Nor could she accept any longer the way he had so callously deceived her.

And now, six months after signing the final divorce papers, she was embarking on a new life in a new town, where she hoped to regain her health as well as heal the still tender wounds on her usually irrepressible spirit.

When she emerged from the bathroom, tying her robe in place, she found Merry busy adding special touches to the room. A bowl of oranges stood on one bedside table, and a stack of brand-new magazines covered the other. Merry had hung Cynthia's travel outfit in the closet and was now carefully turning back the bed.

"Thanks for all your help," Cynthia said, "but I really don't expect such service. I'm not a paying guest."

"I was told you're a special friend of Mr. Fielding's," Merry said with a smile that further widened her tawny face. "That's why I want to make sure your room is just right."

"Do you like working here?" Cynthia asked as she began to dress.

"We all like working for Mr. Fielding. He's a very nice man. Fun to work for. Always pleasant," she said in a low, melodious voice.

"I'm hoping to find work here soon, myself," Cynthia explained, pulling on a pair of navy-blue gabardine slacks that she'd recently purchased. Everything else she owned was loose and baggy on her since she'd shrunk to an underweight size five during the emotional turmoil of the past year. "If there's something I can do around here to earn my keep, I'll stay and enjoy this beautiful desert climate."

"I hope you'll be here for a good long while," Merry said as she folded an extra blanket from the closet across the foot of the bed. "Mr. Fielding would like that, I'm sure. He *acts* like a happy man. He smiles and laughs all the time. But I think he's very lonely."

"Lonely?" Cynthia wondered how any man married to outgoing and fun-loving Helene could be lonely.

"We tease him a lot, the maids and other

6

staff members," Merry continued. "We all think he needs someone to share that beautiful house on the top of the hill with him. We ask him when such a handsome bachelor is going to find himself a wife."

"Find a wife?" Cynthia exclaimed. Her hands stopped in midair, where they had been buttoning up her lightblue silk blouse. "But Russ Fielding isn't a bachelor. He's married. I knew him when he got engaged to Helene. I was there when they planned the wedding."

"Oh, you mean Helene Vickers," Merry said with a short laugh that expressed no real amusement. "Mr. Fielding says he's going to grow old waiting for her, but I think he's making a bad joke. He shouldn't wait for her. She's too busy ever to settle down and make a home for him." The young woman's dark eyes clouded as she continued thoughtfully, "He must care for her very much, and that's too bad. My people have a saying – a man who waits too long gets a patient nature as his reward, and that's all."

"Are you telling me Russ and Helene never got married? Why, that's unbelievable! She never wrote me about it."

Now that Cynthia stopped to think about it, she realized Helene had never written much at all. She had sent Chuck and Cynthia a wedding invitation, then a year late she'd sent a copy of the glossy brochure with color photographs of the new Haven Hills Tennis Ranch. Then came a series of postcards from exotic places where she'd apparently been traveling. But she'd never written newsy letters and certainly nothing explaining that the wedding plans had gone awry.

Cynthia had never considered Helen's lack of correspondence particularly odd. She assumed her friend was miffed because she and Chuck had moved to Chicago before graduation, thereby breaking their promise to be in Tucson for Russ and Helene's wedding.

Merry Spring seemed anxious to convince Cynthia. "Miss Vickers comes to the ranch now and then when she isn't off on a trip somewhere. They still see each other. But Mr. Fielding and Miss Vickers are *not* married."

"I just can't believe this!" Cynthia said, trying to absorb the unsettling news as she fastened a gold chain around her neck with trembling fingers. "They seemed so perfect together, so much alike. And, of course, when I saw the pictures of the ranch and realized they'd built it just as they wanted, I assumed they'd made all their dreams come true. It never occurred to me that they might not be married. After all, Helene's father owns all this desert property."

"And Mr. Vickers owns this guest ranch. But he's a good friend of Mr. Fielding's. Mr. Vickers has been like a father to him, Mr. Fielding always says, because he gave him this chance to build up Haven Hills," Merry explained.

"Oh, I'm so glad you told me all this. I might have said something really stupid before Russ got a chance to explain. What if I'd dashed up that hill to the house expecting to be met by Helene? That's really what I pictured, you see. I came here thinking I could get a job helping Helen with her ranch duties. I thought she might have too much to do, being a wife and a full-time partner in this operation, as well."

Merry gave a gentle chuckle. "Miss Vickers is only busy having fun. She has no interest in this place except when there's a party or something. Well, I have to go. I have other rooms to clean

9

before dinner time."

"Thank you, Merry, for staying to talk to me," Cynthia said warmly. "I feel like I've already made a friend in Arizona. And I think I'm going to need one," she added, thinking about how different her visit here was going to be from what she had expected.

All she could think about now was seeing Russ and hearing why his seemingly perfect college romance had never blossomed into the marriage everyone had expected. What had happened between Russ and Helene? Which one of them had called off the wedding at the last minute? And was Russ really waiting around for Helene to change her mind and marry him? Perhaps he'd taken on the job of developing the guest ranch for her father just so he'd be close to Helene, in a convenient position to resume their engagement if she ever gave up her world travels and settled down.

Cynthia checked herself quickly in the mirror. She didn't want to waste time with the curling iron right now, so, hoping her hair still looked perky, she ran a comb through her thick chestnut locks, which now had only slight waves. Her gray eyes stood out like large, luminous circles on her pale face, which was typical of someone with asthma. Her eyes had traces of a wide-open look of panic, and she hoped the effect upon people who met her was winsome rather than unhealthy, as it seemed to her. She applied bright coral blusher to her cheeks to draw attention away from her overly bright eyes and headed for the door.

Her room was located in one of two long buildings that extended outward from the main office toward the swimming pool. Beyond the border of squat red-tile-roofed buildings and green lawns, the ranch was surrounded by flat desert, the monotony broken by the occasional upward thrust of a rocky foothill. In the distance three surrounding mountain ranges rose abruptly. On the way from the airport the station-wagon driver had explained to Cynthia that the ranch was ideally situated on a high desert plateau at the base of the Catalina, the Rincon, and the Tanque Verde mountain ranges. The hills shone multicolored in the bright afternoon sun, with pinkish hues turning to purple and then dark blue in the distance.

Cynthia hurried down carefully manicured paths, encountering several ranch guests and staff members who greeted her with friendly hellos. She smiled and nodded, enjoying the informal atmosphere of the Southwest that she'd heard so much about. She took deep breaths of the life-giving desert air and felt the easy response of her fragile lungs. She knew that after a short time in this healthy climate her asthma would be considered relieved. Here she would suffer no long bouts with the bronchial chest colds that had plagued her during the five winters she'd endured in the Midwest. Here in this peaceful and protected valley she would get well again, physically and spiritually. She was confident that her old energy and enthusiasm would return.

When she'd arrived this afternoon, the driver had also pointed out Russ's home – a modern house of harshly chiseled stone perched on a sharp promontory overlooking the ranch. Now, its broad windows reflected the orange rays of the afternoon sun.

Cynthia had to pause often during the tiring walk up the steep driveway marked PRIVATE which twisted up the hill to the house. She was happy to have an opportunity to look down from the various vantage points. She could see the overall plan and she remembered how years ago Russ had sketched it out on a cocktail napkin for her and Chuck after a tennis game. He'd crossed out the stables and moved them across the property to a gully he'd drawn with a thatching of quick strokes. Now she was looking at the reality, the serene haven he'd created out of the desert.

How had Russ accomplished so much when his personal life had been so disrupted? Cynthia wondered. For canceling the marriage must have caused a flurry of consternation and last-minute changes in people's plans. Had Russ's sunny disposition and openly affectionate nature survived the tumult of the intervening years?

Cynthia arrived at the top of the hill and knocked on the huge carved-wood door. Within seconds it flew out from under her knuckles, and Russ burst onto the front porch, his arms stretched wide for a big hug – just as if they'd seen each other last week instead of five years ago.

"Cynthia, honey! Come and give your old buddy a big hello," he cried in a familiar drawl that stirred her memories

13

of the past.

Before moving into his arms, she stared at him with disbelief for just a moment. He was the same old Russ, but somehow totally different, too. He was a few years older, of course, but that hadn't altered his youthful blond appeal. It had merely added a few laugh lines around his eyes, a heartier musculature to his tall frame, and a leathery tan to his smiling face. No, what had transformed him was his jaunty air of confidence, the evident awareness of his own mature self-sufficiency, which he had not yet acquired as a college boy. He'd been the perfect sunny-faced, long-legged colegiate then, but now he was a man. What he had accomplished here in building the guest ranch had obviously turned him into a satisfied and happy person.

Russ glowed with a contagious vitality. Cynthia threw herself into his waiting arms and he lifted her up off her feet so easily that she was afraid he would toss her up into the air. He planted several hearty kisses of welcome on her cheeks, her nose, and one ear before finally lowering her back to her feet.

"Oh, I'm so glad to see you, you handsome thing," she cried out warmly. 'I

14

always did say you were the most gorgeous man on campus."

She leaned back to stare up into his sky-blue eyes, which reflected the wide-open horizons of Arizona, not the musty and overcast skies she had left behind her. His eyes alone gave her as much hope for the future as did the hot afternoon sunlight that made her body tingle with warmth under her light blouse. Russ kept her imprisoned in a tight bear hug as he led her into the entry hall. He reached out with a shiny cowboy boot and nudged the door closed behind them.

"I'm as happy as can be to get you out here in this healthy climate of ours, Cynthia," he said. "Ever since I got your letter I've been worried sick about you. Why you two ever ran off to live in Chicago I'll never know. You should have stayed right there in your home town, Denver, where you were always perky as a young colt. But don't you worry, we'll take good care of you here." He teased her with another ticklish kiss on her cheek.

"Why, you devil! Now I know what's different about you." She laughed up into his face. "You've grown a moustache! Why, you look like one of those desperados

15

on a WANTED poster in a western movie,"
she said, enjoying the ringing sound of his
laughter in response.

"Do you like it?" he asked, taking up
one edge of the blond thatch above his
mouth and twirling it with a phony
malevolent grin.

"I think so," she said hestitantly,
studying the contrast between his straight
blond hair and the lightly curling hairs on
his upper lip that made him look more
handsome than the Sundance Kid. "I just
have to get used to it," she said. "I'll bet
Helene loves it."

Ignoring the opening she'd given him in
mentioning his former fiancée's name,
Russ leaned around to kiss her neck just
above her silky collar. She giggled as the
wiry brush of his moustache bristled along
her sensitive skin.

"I'm glad to see you, little darlin'. I
didn't expect you quite so early," he said,
moving his provocative attention from her
neck to her wide gray eyes. "I just this
minute got out of the shower." He began
tucking in his shirt of pale green cotton,
which had a pattern of darker green stitches
across the decorated yoke. His skin-tight
blue jeans revealed every muscle in

his lean thighs.

"The man who picked me up at the airport told me you wanted me to come up here for dinner," Cynthia explained. "And I was so eager to start catching up on the news with you that here I am!"

Russ reached over and patted her shoulder with casual affection. How reassuring it felt to fall so easily back into the habits of warm friendship with him! She moved down a few steps into the living room.

"Your house is beautiful," she said, admiring the decor. Colorful Indian rugs hung from the walls, a bronze statue of a bucking bronco was prominently displayed on a stand under a beam of light, and massive leather couches and chairs offered comfortable-looking resting places that might be suitable for raw-boned cow punchers. This was clearly not a room designed for the very feminine Helene.

"The perfect bachelor hideaway," Cynthia said pointedly, turning to look over her shoulder at Russ, waiting for him to explain his marital status. But instead he turned the conversation back to her with a question that shocked her.

"Where's Chuck?" he asked. "Didn't

your husband come with you?"

Cynthia was stupefied. Didn't he know? "Russ, didn't Helene tell you? Chuck and I are divorced. I wrote her all about it." Now Cynthia wondered just how much contact Russ had had with Helene recently.

Now it was Russ's turn to stare at her in shock. "You two are *divorced?* But you always seemed so compatible." He seemed truly shaken by the news.

"A great deal has happened to change those glowing plans we made during our college days," Cynthia said. "I'm sure you understand. The real world can toss you around, twist things, destroy your three-tier-wedding-cake expectations."

"I think I need a drink, don't you?" Russ muttered, turning away from her. The comforting good cheer that had radiated from him earlier suddenly dimmed. His welcoming words now sounded forced, as if he were overplaying the role of congenial host in order to conceal his sock at hearing something unpleasant.

"We need some fresh air. Follow me, honey. Out west you'll find we do everything outside. Yes, I said everything!" he said with an overly hearty

18

laugh. He opened a sliding glass door that led to the patio. "I'm going to make you a strawberry margarita you'll never forget."

"That sounds good," Cynthia said, glad to agree to any drink that would take him a while to fix. She wanted to give him time to adjust to what she'd just told him.

But as soon as he stepped behind the tile counter that served as an outdoor cooking area, he seemed to forget all about the drinks and leaned over to stare at her intently. "Damn it, Cynthia," he burst out, "I was afraid you'd push that man of yours too far someday."

His unfair attack made Cynthia freeze with sudden anger. "Is that what you think? Then you're crazy! I didn't push Charles Price around!"

"I happen to think differently," Russ said, straightening up to his full height of well over six feet and rocking backwards on his heels, his arms crossed on his chest in a stubborn stance.

"Well, it won't be the first time we've disagreed about something," she said crossly.

"I knew Chuck couldn't live up to your ambitions, that one day he'd rebel," Russ said.

"Why, that's not what happened at all! You don't understand. Of course I wanted the best for my husband. I wanted him to get ahead in the world and be happy. That's only natural. But our marriage certainly wasn't spoiled by *my* overambition."

"A man needs to feel that he's the one in charge, that he can make his own decisions," Russ continued doggedly. The slanting orange beams of the sunset behind Cynthia were reflected in his light eyes, tinging his usually cool demeanor with aggression. "Look how you talked him into that job in Chicago."

"But he never listened to me about anything. Believe me! *Chuck* decided to go to work for that plastics company. He never even told me he was looking for work until he announced that we were leaving school a few days before graduation so he could take the job. He was determined to beat out all the applicants getting out of school in June. He didn't care that we'd miss the graduation ceremony or the vacation trip to Tucson that he'd promsied me. All he could think about was his important career."

"You seemed happy enough with his

decision at the time," Russ countered.

"That's only because I was trying desperately to be a dutiful wife. What I wanted was for him to go on to graduate school and get a business degree. I didn't push him into taking the first job that came along."

When Russ still looked unconvinced and began dispiritedly tossing ingredients into a blender for their drinks, she tried to conclude their disagreement with the most telling point for her side.

"Do you think that with my asthma I'd ever have chosen to live in Chicago? You're wrong if you think I ran Chuck's life."

The noisy whir of the blender blotted out further conversation. Russ filled two large goblets and looked up at Cynthia as if trying to assess what she'd told him. A determined smile erased the stubborn lines of resistance from his face.

"Come on now, enough of this subject," he said, handing her a glass. "We're getting into one of those unresolvable controversies, just like we used to in college." His tone was softer now, as if he were no longer interested in assigning blame for the breakup of Cynthia's marriage. "What's done is done," he

21

added, "and why it happened doesn't matter. I guess it's just hard for me to picture you sitting back and letting someone else run your life for you. Remember how I always called you the little busybody? You were always bustling about making plans for everyone, keeping us all superorganized and supermotivated."

"Can I help it if I was born with a lot of energy?" Cynthia smiled back at him, hoping to reestablish their easy verbal jousting, which had kept their talks lively in the old days. They had argued about almost everything then, but the topics had been less personal, less likely to hurt someone.

"Oh, is that what you call it? Energy?" Russ asked with a casual lift of his shoulders as he came out from behind the bar. He took a lusty swallow of his drink, then smiled again. 'Well, all I know is that so much enthusiasm can exhaust everyone around you. And out here in ranch country we like to take things easy."

"Are you warning me to slow down?" Cynthia asked, eyeing him over the rim of the glass as she took a taste of the tart drink.

Russ lowered his voice to a more intimate

tone that commanded all her attention. "Yes, I am, Cynthia. For your own good. You may have ruined your marriage, and you may have ruined your health by letting loose all of that so-called energy."

Cynthia turned away from him and walked over to the porch swing that was suspended from a patio trellis. She sat down carefully, trying not to spill her drink.

She refused to listen to any more of Russ's suggestions on how to readjust her personality. When her divorce was pending she had spent months dwelling on her own shortcomings. She'd been haunted by the guilty feeling that she had caused the marriage to fail, that there must be something about her she could change in order to save the relationship. She should be less idealistic and teach herself to live with a man she didn't trust. Or she should harden herself so she wouldn't be hurt when he lied to her. But the prospect of living the rest of her life with a man for whom she had no respect had, in the end, convinced her that the marriage was hopeless.

Now she had come to Arizona, drawn by the instinctive feeling that Russ and

Helene's carefree attitude and relaxed manner might rub off on her, might help her to start a new and more lighthearted lifestyle. She had pictured herself grabbing onto the coattails of their happiness and success, no longer moping about what she'd done wrong, where she'd gone off track. But she couldn't get the solace and inspiration from Russ that she needed if he continued to avoid telling her about his breakup with Helene. As he came over to sit beside her on the plump cushions of the swing, she decided to give him another opening.

"I'm sorry my divorce came as such a surprise to you," she began. "I'd assumed Helene had told you about it."

"She never mentioned it."

"Well, I know she's been gone a lot. She's sent me postcards from Paris, Madrid, Tokyo. She loves to travel, doesn't she?"

"Yes, she does. I only see her between trips."

"I was hoping she'd be here tonight. Is she away on a trip right now?" Cynthia pressed.

"She's in New York, I think."

"That must leave you short-handed here

on the ranch," Cynthia commented after releasing a tense sigh. How many times would he dodge the issue?

"Oh, no." He laughed casually. "Helene doesn't do much around here."

Cynthia placed her empty glass on the redwood table beside her. Her breath was coming in short, impatient gasps of increasing anger. Why did he refuse to discuss his relationship with Helene? Didn't he realize how unfair it was to leave her in the dark this way, unable to converse honestly wth him?

"Calm down, will you Cynthia? You look as tense as a cowgirl sitting on her first wild mustang," Russ told her. "This is an evening to be savored. Now sit back and try to enjoy life for a while."

He reached one long arm toward her and drew her narrow shoulders toward him. She let him pull her into the circle of his embrace. He bent his head down close to hers and said softly near her ear, "I'm sorry for heaping all that criticism on you about your marriage. It just seems to come naturally to me to point out where you're wrong. Remember how we used to go at it in the old days? After playing tennis, you and I would begin by analyzing all the presidential candidates. Chuck and Helene would just sit back and listen while we disagreed on every one of them."

His moustache twitching so close to her cheekbone, delicately brushing the satiny skin of Cynthia's face, gave her an oddly dizzy feeling that made her incapable of concentrating on his apology. Again he was distracting her from the conversational line she wanted to pursue.

With restless annoyance she stood up and walked over to the edge of the patio. Russ followed and placed one arm around her shoulders as if to calm her as she gazed down at the broad expanse of desert floor.

"Everything is more green here than I expected," she said, noticing the hardy plants that seemed to thrive on the arid desert dunes.

"We have an unusually high table of underground water here," Russ said. "In fact, the Indians named this place Tucson because it means 'the spring at the foot of black moutain.' The availablility of well water was the main reason early settlers liked this place."

"It's lovely. Not as desolate as I expected the desert to be. It's beautiful and tranquil."

"Hey, maybe there's hope for you yet," Russ exclaimed. "It takes a special kind of sensitivity to appreciate the beauty of the desert," he said, drawing her closer to him in a congratulatory hug. "And here I considered you a big-city girl. You always preferred downtown Denver to the wilds of the Rocky Mountains nearby."

"I do like city life. There's a lot of variety in a city. You meet all kinds of people."

"Most of them you'd rather not walk more than a block with."

"And on any night you can choose between going to the opera or the symphony or any number of plays."

"But in the country you just walk out your front door and find beauty no composer or writer has ever been able to capture."

"If you like the outdoors, every city has parks to explore," she said, drawing away from his grasp.

"Yes, if you can find a parking place."

"The city is more stimulating than the country. All the people round you provide a clash of ideas."

"That is if the clash of traffic doesn't put you in the hospital on your way to meet these stimulating people."

"Cities are exciting."

"Cities are dirty."

They stood facing one another, their bodies rigid and unyielding.

"Just tell me honestly. Did you love living in Chicago?" Russ asked.

"No!" Cynthia answered quickly. "But that had nothing to do with the place."

"I rest my case," Russ stated, spreading both arms wide before him. "You've chosen the wide-open spaces of Haven Hills over Chicago. Enough said."

He put his arm around Cynthia's shoulders once again. She'd found their brief sparring match invigorating, and felt the calm afterglow of a battle well fought.

Cynthia laughed as she looked down on the outline of the ranch buildings. "All right, Russ, you win, you win. Who wouldn't prefer this wonderland you've created? Everything is perfectly planned, just the way I remember you talking about it."

She stood there thinking, remembering that most of the specifics about the design had been Russ's ideas. Helene had contributed very little after she had initially sparked his interest by suggesting the original plan.

"Have Helene and her father let you set up things just as you like?" Cynthia asked.

"Oh, Max Vickers and I talk everything over," Russ acknowledged. "But he's usually pretty easy to convince."

"Not as easy as Helene, I take it." Cynthia turned to look up at him with a meaningful expression, her frustration making her lean toward him, her breasts beneath the tightly stretched silk almost brushing his wide chest.

"What do you mean, Cynthia?'"

"I mean that there must have been times when you couldn't get Helene to do what you want."

Russell was looking at her with a benign expression. In the deepening twilight his face was dusky, his light eyelashes casting long, flickering shadows across his high cheekbones. His blue eyes had darkened to a deep purple. Cynthia felt a surge of warmth at the back of her neck as she studied him with consternation, waiting for the explanation she felt he owed her.

"I don't know why you keep bringing up Helene," Russ said. "You seem so interested in everything she's doing. I didn't think you two were that close back in the old days." He broke loose from her gaze and looked across the desert toward the darkening horizon. "As a foursome we got along okay on the tennis courts, and maybe going out afterwards. But you and Helene never seemed to have a lot in common to talk about."

That was certainly true. Cynthia and Chuck had played tennis every weekend with Helene and Russ during their senior year of college, and their foursome had become a friendly habit. But Cynthia had always suspected that Helene encouraged the weekly date in the hope that by forming a close alliance with a couple already married she would get closer to Russ Fielding, whom she had been dating only casually when the two couples first began meeting. If that had been her plan, it had worked. Russ and Helene's relationship had deepened into an engagement with plans for the future, as Helene continued to think up clever activities to keep them all busy together.

"I can't help being curious about what's happened to you and Helene since college," Cynthia said in a nervous torrent of words.

"We have all evening for that," Russ objected. "We have to get out some steaks and start up a good fire to cook them on."

He trailed one hand down her arm and took her hand. "Will you come and help me?"

"Of course," she said, returning his smile in spite of her efforts to resist his charm. By now she was hungry enough to let him divert her. Maybe it was better at this point to give up rather than force a confrontation over a subject he was so unwilling to discuss.

She would try again after dinner. They were meeting now as if for the frst time, their situations completely different from when they'd known each other before, when she'd been a hopeful young bride and he'd been firmly committed to another woman. This was a new game with new rules. But until Russ was honest with her and explained fully why he wasn't married, the game could not begin.

Chapter Two

While the steaks sputtered over a pungent mesquite fire, Cynthia followed Russ's instructions and began buttering French bread and fixing a salad.

'Now where else can you see the Milky Way as clearly as that?'' Russell asked her, waving his barbecue fork toward the sky. Cynthia came over to where he was standing and looked up at the awesome spectacle. "Sort of makes you hanker for the day when we can all travel from planet to planet, doesn't it?'' he went on.

"Oh, I think the space program is nonsense," Cynthia blurted out. "If we spent the same amount of money on practical matters, we could feed millions of hungry people and build safer cities for everyone."

"But think of what our accomplishments in space have done for national pride, how they've opened men's eyes to new possibilites."

Cynthia's heartbeat quickened at his

challenge. She moved closer to get her point of view across better.

"But at what cost? Have you seen the space budget? That's paid for by you and me, by the taxpayers."

"But the taxpayers have benefited, too. The aerospace industry is a major employer. It pumps billions of dollars back into the economy," Russ explained, striding up and down the patio with great energy.

"But these days we can't afford any frivolous extras in the national budget."

"Space exploration is no frivolous extra! We *must* explore our environment; that's basic to human nature. And you're forgetting the technical fallout – all the new products we've developed as a result of what we've learned from space research."

"Teflon? All that effort to discover Teflon?"

And so the argument continued. Cynthia became so totally involved that she prepared dinner as if by rote as they tossed the topic back and forth between them. Falling into her old habit of college days, she debated expertly with Russ, matching him point for point and exulting in each victory of logic, even if it were not her own.

But she never quite convinced him, and by the time the steaks were ready they still had not resolved the issue.

"But, Cynthia, you're completely ignoring the issue of national defense. If the other powers advance the military applications of their space projects – Say, you aren't cutting up that lettuce with a knife, are you?"

"We're going to eat the salad right away, so I'm slicing it. The only time it's necessary to tear salad greens with your hands is if you're going to be keeping the salad for a while."

"But I like my salad in big torn chunks," Russ protested, leaning toward her aggressively.

"And I like mine finely shredded, cut with a knife," she retorted, leaning forward from the waist in the same manner, the sharp knife held defensively in front of her.

"Can't we ever agree on anything?" Russ laughed. The rippling sound cut across the cool night, immediately erasing the tension between them.

"I guess not," she consented. Russ's laughter was so infectious that she joined in. "Space! Salads! Life in the big city! You name it, we fight about it."

"Well, I'm going to cook the steaks the way I like them," Russ said, "and you make the salad the way you like it, and we won't argue any more, because obviously we'll never agree on anything. Let's just eat and enjoy."

They sat down to eat at an outdoor table next to the smoldering barbecue pit, talking about old college friends and what they were doing now. Cynthia had written more letters and kept in better touch, so she had many amusing stories to tell about former acquaintances. Before she knew it, they'd finished dinner, and she had helped Russ carry their plates into the kitchen.

It was hard to believe that her day had begun in Chicago, when she'd risen very early in the morning to catch her plane. Now she felt fatigue catching up with her. She tried to stifle a yawn as she glanced at the clock over the sink.

"I'm sorry," she apologized as she caught Russ looking at her. "I'm still running on Chicago time. Back where I come from it's past my bedtime."

Russ yawned back at her. "I wish you wouldn't do that. Whenever I see someone yawn, it makes me sleepy, too. I guess we'd better get you home to bed. You're supposed to be here for a rest."

He put his arm around her and led her to the door. "I'll walk you down the hill. I wouldn't want you to get lost the first night here," he joked.

He set a lazy pace, holding her close to him so that she was forced to walk slowly through the black night. But she enjoyed taking the time to look up at the sky, feeling as if she were renewing an old friendship with the stars. She and Russ spoke little, but their silence was companionable.

Cynthia was glad they'd put aside their disagreement over Chuck and what had caused her marriage to fail. She remembered that years before Russ had enjoyed teasing her about her big plans for her husband's business career and her ambitions for their life together. Russ felt less pressured to make his way in the world, and she'd always told him that was because he was from a family of Texas land owners who had plenty of money. He had no reason to drive himself.

Now she felt they were on their old, easy footing again, where they could disagree on any issue, learn from each other's arguments, see the subject from many different angles, but take none of it personally.

'I've had a wonderful evening,'' she said at her door, meaning every word of it. She felt five years younger, like a college girl who'd spent the evening with a challenging classmate.

Russ looked up over her head. "Look at that. The light over your door is burned out. One more thing to fix." He sighed. "When I have time." He placed his arms around her waist.

"You must have a lot on your mind, lots of responsibilities," Cynthia said as, without thinking, she curved close to him.

"Oh, I don't let it get me down. There's still plenty of time for doing nothing. That's my favorite activity, you know." She felt each word as he breathed it close to her cheek. "Next to tennis and riding and holding pretty girls like you close to me."

Cynthia realized with a start that what had been chummy closeness just a few moments ago was rapidly taking on a new and more dangerous character. Russ was rubbing his hands sensuously across the silky covering on her back, and she felt the prickly path of his moustache across her face and down her neck.

37

"Thank you for dinner, Russ. I think I'd better go inside now," she stammered.

"Without a good-night kiss to sleep on?" he asked her, throwing his head back with a mocking smile so that, even in the darkness, she saw his white teeth glisten in straight rows beneath the golden hair of his upper lip.

Cynthia squirmed uncomfortably within his embrace as she thought furiously of how to escape the disturbing new situation she found herself in. She didn't understand what was happening. She felt uneasy in his arms when there were so many things still unsaid between them.

"Now, Russ, let me go inside. You're the one who wants to help me recover my health. I need lots of sleep, you know. That should do the trick." She gave a nervous laugh that probably sounded as phony as it felt.

But before she could put more sincerity into her voice, the sound was dampened and rumbled into silence in her throat as Russ placed his mouth over hers. In an instant she melted against the warm lips of this man whom she had never let herself dream of kissing.

Russ was a man without urgency,

incapable of rushing something, and too easygoing to ever force an issue. But his kiss had a compelling quality that seemed to draw Cynthia to it and hold her suspended within its quiet power. The stars over her head blinked out, just as the defective light at her door had done, and she was swirling through blackness, caught up in something dark and mysterious that enthralled yet alarmed her.

Without realizing what she was doing, she reached up and placed her hands about his neck, resting her fingers against the base of his hairline. Russ responded to her mute act by intensifying the fervor of his kiss, drawing her so close to him in a crushing embrace that her delicate body seemed endangered yet protected at the same time.

Shock waves were rippling down her body in rapidly intensifying tremors of excitement. She had never dared to consider being held and kissed like this by a man she'd known for so long. She'd never dared to imagine what an assault upon her senses his lips might be. And now, with very little warning, their relationship had been suddenly and forever changed. Never again could she casually accept the affectionate familiarity he had given so easily.

Once she had found innocent fun in flirting with Russ. She had felt safe throwing herself into his arms, receiving his exuberant kisses like a loving sister. Then they'd both been safely tied in commitments to other people. But now she sensed dangers at the end of the road. She could see the precipice over which he might lead her.

"Stop, Russ." She chocked out the words, putting a trembling hand to her lips as she drew away from him.

"I've always wanted to do that " he said, his voice husky. And then he turned suddenly and walked away. For a long time she heard the crunch of his boots across the parking area. But his wide shoulders disappeared into the darkness as she stood touching her face lightly with both hands, looking after him with wonder.

Russ had not kissed her like a good friend. He had given her a kiss with a message, and the message was as old as time itself, and powerful in its implications. Cynthia went into her room and closed the door behind her.

As confusing thoughts raced through her

mind, she mechanically began removing her clothes, hanging up her blouse and slacks and then slipping out of her underwear and into her nightgown.

For a long time she sat on the edge of her bed, remembering that during the entire evening, even as she'd introduced countless references to Helene into the conversation, Russ had never once clarified his relationship with her. He had never told Cynthia that they weren't married or given her a reason why. He'd never explained his continued presence at Haven Hills or told her why he was fulfilling the plans they'd made as a couple even though they had never married.

Without realizing it, Cynthia slowly began to put her clothes back on. She dressed without any specific plan in mind, compelled by a rising tide of anger that put her into a fury of activity.

He should have been honest with her. He should have explained his change in marital plans to her as soon as she told him about her divorce from Chuck, so that they could have reestablished their relationship right then, gotten things out in the open, and decided whether the two of them could be friends or whether the phantom presences

41

of Chuck and Helene would haunt them.

Now Cynthia knew she had to go back to him immediately and talk this out. She couldn't wait any longer. The confrontation was inevitable, and the sooner it came the better. She had to find out if she and Russ had the basis for a new rapport, or if she should leave Haven Hills and try to put him out of her mind forever.

She rushed out into the darkness, so revitalized by her anger that she hardly noticed the steep climb up the hill to Russ's house.

She pounded on the big oak door for several moments before it opened slowly. She leaned forward to peer into the darkness at a shadowy form stretching sleepily awake.

"Cynthia! What's wrong? What brings you back up here to make such a racket at my door and wake me up?" Russ's throaty half-whisper made it clear he'd been asleep.

As she stepped inside, he flicked on a light and her resolve almost melted away with chagrin. He was as disheveled and sleepy eyed as if she'd rolled over in bed and shaken him awake beside her.

"I'm sorry to get you out of bed," she apologized.

"If I had to be awakened, I can't think of anybody I'd rather have do the rousing." He grinned at her lecherously.

He held his arms out toward her as she strode past him, just as he had several times already that evening, but she refused to let his embrace defuse her determination. She marched into the high-ceilinged living room, knowing she was no longer safe within his arms, knowing she couldn't go there as if to a calm refuge. Now the sight of him, naked from the waist up, wearing only loosely fastened pajama bottoms that looked like they might slip off at any moment, seemed very threatening, the invitation to an adventure too daring to consider.

"We have to talk, Russ, and I'd just as soon be across the room from you while we do it," she said calmly. "Especially when you're dressed – or undressed – the way you are."

His grin faded and his arms dropped. "Well, if I can't turn you on," he said with a drowsy slur, "then I think I'll go turn on my old friend the coffee pot. Looks like this is going to be a long night."

When he returned to the room a moment later, she looked up from where she was sitting, feeling terribly small huddled on his giant leather couch.

"Do you suppose you could go put a robe on?" she asked almost shyly.

"I don't own a robe. We desert rats rarely need them."

"I could wait while you get dressed." The sight of his astonishingly broad chest, smoothly hairless and as tanned as calfskin, was disturbing to her, and the pajamas still seemed in imminent danger of slipping off his narrow hips.

"Just go ahead and tell me what has you so worked up that you'd come charging up the hill like this in the middle of the night," he said, and then yawned.

"Oh, all right," she said, looking away from him and wetting her dry lips nervously. "I want to know why you didn't tell me you and Helene never got married. I wrote to you assuming I'd be coming to visit the two of you. It was only when I got here that I found out the wedding never took place."

"Helene never wrote you about it?" When Cynthia gave a solemn shake of her head, he continued, "I knew she had your phone number in Chicago. I was sure she would call and tell you or Chuck all about

44

it." He absently rubbed one hand across his flat stomach, then continued. "She had a lot of explaining to do just to her friends here in Tucson. You have to understand Helene. She's not like you Cynthia. She's very immature, and if there's something she doesn't want to do, she simply avoids it."

"Well, I think you should have explained to me earlier this evening what happened to your wedding plans. I gave you plenty of openings."

"How it all happened isn't exactly my favorite topic of conversation. I assumed you already knew about it. Just as you assumed I already knew about your divorce."

"It seems Helene hasn't been a very reliable means of communication," Cynthia said with a tenuous smile. Finally she was beginning to understand the ridiculous mix-up that had kept her perplexed and increasingly frustrated most of the evening.

"I think from now on we'd better just tell each other directly anything we have to say," Russ said. "For starters, what are you thinking right now? Your eyes have dimmed to the color of storm clouds."

"I was just thinking how I'll have to

45

change my plans. I thought I was coming out here to visit old friends, a happily married couple that was offering me a place to live when I needed one. I hoped I could get well here and help Helene with her work. But now I think I'd better leave."

Russ rose from the couch across from her and started forward, then apparently thought better of it and stopped to stand facing her, an earnest expression on his face.

"I want you to stay on here, just as you planned," he said firmly. "This is the perfect place to recuperate, and I've had my heart set on playing tennis with you and sunning with you. I've been planning this rehabilitation program since I got your letter."

"I don't know, Russ," she began, trying to adjust to the rapid change of events.

Russ turned toward the kitchen and disappeared, calling to her, "You aren't going anywhere right this minute. We're going to have a cup of coffee and talk about it."

When he came back a few minutes later and placed a tray on the coffee table in front of her, Cynthia noticed that he'd changed into a pair of soft faded jeans that were only slightly less revealing than the pajamas he had been wearing. He was still shirtless, and Cynthia found herself admiring the smooth, golden sheen and prominent muscles of his chest. He had perfect skin that cried out for an appreciative touch. She gripped both hands on her lap in front of her, wondering why they trembled as she thought of trailing them languidly across that amber warmth.

Russ must have noticed something in her anticipatory look, her head thrown back so that her velvety brown hair dropped straight down onto her shoulders, the heat of a blush making its way up her neck and across her face. He stood still, not speaking, watching her with an interested smile, one eyebrow rising slowly into an arch that turned his face into an unspoken question.

She had to stop fantasizing like this now that she and Russ were both single and available, she told herself. It wasn't like the old days, when their attitudes toward each other had been strictly limited by social convention. This was a more dangerous game, one for which she had no rules to help guide her. And she wasn't sure she was in any condition to play. Not after what she'd been through with Chuck, not after she'd been stripped of all her trust in the opposite sex.

Like a splash of unexpected rain, thoughts of the past chilled her, and she lunged forward for the cup of coffee almost forgotten in front of her.

"Come and get it while it's hot," she urged Russ, regretting almost at once her unfortunate choice of words. He gave her an exaggerated double take, deliberately misunderstanding.

She thought of the years before, when they'd known each other as casual weekend tennis opponents. Their friendship had indeed been cool then. But as she reached out for the coffee cup and found it still warm to the touch, she realized that everything was different now – and the change was going to take some getting used to. They both had to reassess their formerly easy and thoughtless enjoyment of each other, for more serious consequences had now become a possibility. Whether she stayed on here for a few days vacation or for the entire winter season, it was going to be a far different visit than she had expected.

She tried to distract them both from the tension building between them by asking questions. "So, will you please explain how Haven Hills Tennis Ranch ever got built on Mr. Vickers's property if you and Helene didn't get married as planned? And how you happen to be living here, in charge of things, even though you aren't Mr. Vickers's son-in-law?"

Russ sat down on the couch across from her and threw his legs up onto the glass-topped coffee table between them. "Because Helene's dad is a great guy, that's why. He liked my ideas for the ranch and was convinced I was the best one to see them through. Even when the wedding was called off, he insisted I stay on."

"And you agreed?" Cynthia asked with some surprise.

"I had no better alternative. I thought about my brothers living off my grandfather's money in Texas, doing nothing, just waiting for their inheritance. And I realized that if I went back there, I'd do the same thing, and I'd never have a chance to prove myself. There wouldn't be any challenge living off a family ranch that was running just fine without me. But here I could build something of my own, accomplish something. The choice was easy."

"Did Helene mind you staying on here, working so closely with her father?" Cynthia noticed that Russ had never explained which one of them had called off the wedding. If Helene had, she might not have wanted Russ around. Maybe that explained why she spent so much time traveling.

"No, things are very friendly. She lives in town with her father, and I see her from time to time when she's in Tucson. I try to be available when she needs me," he concluded, his light eyes turning shades darker as he pushed his streaked blond hair out of his eyes.

"I'm glad there's no bitterness between you and Helene," Cynthia said flatly, thinking about the angry accusations and painful bitterness that had accompanied her separation from Chuck. "And you're lucky to have become such good friends with Mr. Vickers."

"You know, my father died when I was young, and my brothers and I were raised by my grandfather, who was too old or too busy or too remote to be much of an influence on me. But I've loved Max Vickers since the day I showed up in his den to meet him and officially ask for his

50

daughter's hand in marriage. That was right after graduation, when I came to Tucson with Helene. What happened afterward didn't change that bond between Max and me."

"What did happen?" Cynthia asked cautiously. She didn't want to pry if the subject was painful, but Russ seemed to find talking about it easy, and she thought he seemed relieved to have an old friend to share it with.

"The wedding was all planned, the invitations were out."

"Yes, I remember we received one in Chicago. I sent a note saying we couldn't get here for it as we'd hoped."

"Then one night we got in a terrible ruckus that went on until very late – right in the living room of her father's house. I'm sure her father heard us shouting at each other. He probably didn't sleep very much that night. The next morning Helene was on the phone calling up the caterers, the florists; the wedding was off."

"But you stayed on. You seem very content with life at Haven Hills."

"Yes. It's funny. If Helene had married me, I'd own the place, I guess. As it is, I'm just the resident manager and tennis coach.

But I'm happy. It's a soft life now that everything's all set up. The place almost runs itself," he concluded, with the languorous timbre to his voice that she remembered so well.

"But things have certainly turned out differently for both of us than we expected when we were naive college kids," Cynthia commented, feeling depressed. "Things seemed so simple then." She took another sip of coffee, but it had lost the hot richness of the first few swallows, and by now it was only a lukewarm imitation of what coffee should be. She put the cup down and stood up. "But I'm glad to see you can smile through it all, Russ. You never let anything get you down for long."

Russ unfolded his long legs and rose to face her. "There's nothing to get me down. My life is fine, just fine. Especially now that you're here to keep me company and remind me of the good ol' days."

Again Cynthia felt an uncomfortable tremor inside as she thought of what Russ might expect from her now that they were meeting on an entirely new basis. And she knew her fear made her want to leave as soon as possible. She moved away from Russ, toward the safety of the door, her heart beating rapidly beneath the soft silk blouse.

"I think I should make some travel arrangements tomorrow, Russ. I don't feel right about staying here as your guest indefinitely, sponging off of you."

"We can find work for you to do. Meet me for breakfast and we'll talk about it."

"Well, one thing's for sure. It's too late to talk about it tonight," she agreed, stretching her tired arms over her head as she walked toward the door.

Without warning, Russ reached out from behind her and grabbed her around the waist, pulling her backward against him, catching her with her arms still up in the air.

"Would you like to make that breakfast in bed tomorrow?" he said seductively next to her cheek as she twisted about in his arms, desperate to escape his overpowering presence. She needed time to think. He was asking too much of her too quickly.

"Breakfast in bed?" She lowered her hands hesitantly to his bare shoulders.

"Yes, you could stay here with me tonight, and if you are a very good girl, you might be served breakfast in bed."

"Please, Russ, don't tease me. We knew

each other a long time ago, but right now we're practically strangers. Do you understand what I mean?"

"Then let's start getting acquainted," he said, closing his eyes and rubbing his rough cheek against her smooth one.

She shook her head slightly, spinning a cloud of chestnut-colored hair into his face. He laughed softly and reached up with one hand to gather her hair into a bunch, then pulled her head back so that she was forced to look directly up at him. Her lips parted involuntarily as she studied the rugged planes of his face with rapt fascination. Every feature was familiar to her, yet he was a stranger. His eyes sparkled with desire. She'd never seen the smoldering blue flames in his eyes or the hungry anticipation that made his tongue dart quickly across his lips as his face came closer to hers.

But he kissed her with incredible gentleness. Russ seemed to be tentatively exploring her pliant lips, requesting her permission to delve further. His touch was as polite and respectful as a handshake in a business office, his hands lightly encircling her waist. He was not rushing her, in no way trying to exert the full force of his passion to overcome her objections. He was seducing her with his very absence of demand.

She relaxed enough to place her hands flat on the tantalizing skin of his upper chest, and soon found her fingers moving over him, investigating with delight the muscled shapes she had admired earlier. Her sensitive fingertips continued to glide over the warm skin, up over his shoulders and onto his upper back, where she felt the lacing of new and more sinewy tendons just beneath the surface.

But before their embrace could progress into the more provocative lovemaking his kiss was requesting, he pulled his lips from hers, leaving her breathlessly wishing for more. With exquisite timing he was curtailing their quest for pleasure, just when she might have consented to more. Her earlier resistance had dissolved, and she remained pliant within his arms as she tried to sort out her feelings. He was tantalizing her, trying to seduce her into his world, where affection was natural and expected, where lovemaking was as casual as a wave hello or goodbye.

'Is eight o'clock too early for you?'' he whispered, and for a moment she was too dazed to understand.

"Eight o'clock? You mean for breakfast tomorrow? Yes, that's fine."

"Then I'll meet you in the dining room. Sleep well," he said, brushing a kiss lightly across her forehead before releasing his hold on her.

At the door she ducked under his arm where he'd braced it against the jamb. He made no attempt to hold her, but she thought she heard his laughter even as the door closed, and she scurried out into the night.

Once she was on her way down the hill again, she felt strangely exhilarated by Russell's kiss. She almost skipped along in the dark. It felt good to be looked at with admiration again. It felt good to be stirred by the teasing promise in Russ Fielding's blue eyes. She was tempted to throw all caution aside. A new and unexpected desire was stirring within her, and she was intrigued to know where it would lead her.

But when she arrived back at her room she reminded herself that she mustn't be fooled into thinking she was twenty years old again. A lot had changed and she was very different. She could no longer pursue the simple pleasures that others took for granted, for she had tasted the bitterness of love lost. She knew the risks. Perhaps she could never again seek out with carefree joy the happy stimulation that Russ Fielding offered her.

The next morning Cynthia was still torn between wanting to stay in Tucson and feeling she should go. She dressed for breakfast, putting on the only cotton dress she owned, a conservative dark plaid she'd worn to the office during the uncomfortable Chicago summers.

After serving as bookkeeper for years, she'd become office manager of a large insurance agency. She knew she would be welcomed back to that busy office if that's what she decided to do. Or perhaps she could live in the little house in Denver that her mother shared with her widowed sister. These alternatives, however unappealing, would certainly leave her life less disrupted than would sharing fun in the sun with Russ here at Haven Hills.

Cynthia was still preoccupied with her thoughts when she found Russ waiting for her near the entrance to the dining room. He guided her to a table for two at the back of the room, away from the chattering guests, who were passing around enormous platters of food and discussing their plans for the day with great animation.

"I was hoping you'd be wearing your tennis clothes so we could have a game this morning," he said cheerily. "I always loved playing against you." He chuckled. "You'd dash back and forth just like Chuck, and Helene and I would just stay in our places on the other side of the net and wait for you to wear yourselves out. Then we'd win the match in the last few minutes with no effort at all."

"Oh, yes," she agreed, "I remember the strategy very well. You two just lounged around, barely exerting any effort at all, while Chuck and I played until we were exhausted. I always thought we were badly paired. It would have been a better match if Chuck and Helene had played you and me."

Cynthia was appalled as soon as she realized what she'd said, but she darted a quick glance at Russ and saw with relief that his face was expressionless. As he seated her at the table, he seemed to be distracted and gave no indication he'd heard her.

Of course, both she and Russ had been

matched perfectly with their respective partners, Cynthia insisted to herself. They had both been attracted to people just like themselves. But that made them mismatched in doubles tennis, with two ambitious, hard-working types – Chuck and Cynthia – on one side of the net, and two easygoing types – Helene and Russ – across from them. They would have played better with one of each type on each team.

But Cynthia didn't give into the temptation to carry that thought into real life. Although she and Russ might have made a winning doubles tennis team, their personalities were so different that they had never stopped arguing off the courts. For romance and marriage two people needed similar goals and lifestyles. Such as she and Chuck had had. Such as Helene and Russ had shared.

"What were you saying about our tennis partnerships?" Russ said, handing her a menu.

"Oh, I don't know, I've forgotten," she said, relaxing. "Now, let's see. I guess I'll just have my usual coffee and juice," she told the waitress.

"Oh no you don't," Russ protested. "Sarah, bring us both the breakfast special—three fried eggs, bacon, and a stack of hot cakes."

"Yes, sir," the waitress said, leaving a pitcher of juice on the table.

"I can't eat all that," Cynthia protested.

"Sweetheart, I've put myself in charge of your recovery, and I intend to start by fleshing out that pretty little form of yours with some luscious curves."

"I've waited all my life to be slender like this, and you want to ruin it!" she exclaimed in mock horror. But for some reason – perhaps the blazing sunshine slanting through the windows, her cheerful breakfast companion, or the enticing smells of maple syrup and frying bacon – Cynthia's appetite was stirred. As she gulped down a glass of freshly squeezed orange juice, she realized she was famished.

She caught Russ looking distastefully at her dark, drab dress. "You can change for tennis, and then, after our game, I'll take you into town so you can buy some new clothes. We have more than 3,800 hours of sunshine here every year. You can't walk around in those dreary duds all winter."

"If I stay, that is," she said, still uncertain as to what to do. Even early in the morning his powerful masculinity had a

60

disturbing effect on her.

"I'm going to assume that you're staying," Russ said, challenging her with a riveting look. "Besides, where would you go from here?"

"I could go back to Chicago or to Denver. But now that I've sampled this wonderful desert climate, it would be hard to leave Arizona," she admitted, her gray eyes appreciatively scanning the sunny ranch scene outside the window. "I'm an experienced bookkeeper. Maybe I could find a job in Tucson."

Russ leaned forward in his chair, propping his elbows on the table and folding his large hands together. "You can have a job right here. I told you that."

"I don't want you to dig up some silly little makework project for me, just to keep me busy and make me think I'm earning my own way."

At that moment, the waitress arrived with their food, and Cynthia began pouring syrup over her hot cakes.

"You haven't been well. You should devote yourself to a full-time rest," Russ admonished her. "You shouldn't even think about work."

"I'm feeling better already. Just being

able to breathe this air will improve my condition in a hurry," Cynthia said between mouthfuls. "You can't imagine how wonderful it will be for me to get through a winter without an attack of bronchitis." She began salting and peppering her eggs enthusiastically.

"Will you at least forget those travel plans for today and stay over and enjoy a little sun time with me?" Russ pleaded.

Cynthia nodded. "I'd like that," she agreed after swallowing a delicious bite of bacon.

Russ settled back in his chair and began eating his own breakfast. Cynthia noticed that his mouth twitched slightly beneath his moustache. He seemed happy to have won this concession and acted as though the battle was over.

"After I order you another stack of hot cakes, we'll decide on a time for that tennis game," Russ said, laughter coloring his voice. He waved across the room to their waitress, and before long three great round pancakes materialized on a fresh plate beside Cynthia.

"When I finish eating – "

"*If* you ever finish eating," Russ corrected her.

"I'd like a tour of the place," she finished, ignoring him. "Let's start with the tennis courts first, then see the stables, the main lounge, and the pool – then I'd like to hear all about your plans for the future."

Russ sipped his coffee, shooting her a look of disappointment over his cup. "No tennis game? No leisurely drive into town for sightseeing and shopping? Is that all you ever want to do, talk business, discuss plans? Can't you relax and enjoy life?"

"I happen to enjoy keeping busy. And besides, this beautiful, warm morning has given me a burst of energy." Cynthia discreetly licked maple syrup from her fingers. "I want to tour every nook and cranny of the place and hear all about it," she said, sitting up straight in her chair and clutching the edge of the table in her eagerness to get going.

"I don't know," Russ said, leaning back and refusing to be hurried. "Maybe having you around won't be as much fun as I thought," he said with an exaggerated grin that made it plain he wasn't serious. "I pictured tennis games and sipping margaritas by the pool and political discussions in front of the fire, and all you

63

want to do is talk business."

"You know that's my nature, Russ. It always has been, even during my illness. And it always will be. Now, will you show me around?"

"Oh, I guess it will do me good to stretch my legs a bit," Russ drawled, obviously more interested in lingering over several cups of coffee.

"Now I haven't said I'm going to stay, remember. I just want to look around and see what you've built here."

"Oh, I realize we haven't won you over yet, that Haven Hill Tennis Ranch is only on probation as far as you're concerned. You're probably the hardest customer I've ever had to convince." He took her arm, laughing happily, and guided her across the dining room, stopping on the way to give friendly greetings to several visiting families.

Outside, she noticed that, as they walked around the grounds, Russ continued to respond easily to his guests. Every once in a while an employee or guest would shout hello to him and come rushing up to pull him aside and tell him the latest bawdy joke they'd heard. He'd laugh heartily, his head tipped back as if he was crowing toward the sky. Only then did they resume their tour.

Russell was clearly master of the place, and thoroughly content in his role here. Cynthia hoped to find a place someday where she fit in as comfortably.

When they got to the tennis area, Cynthia was surprised to find that there were only three courts with a tiny pro shop directly behind them with rackets and extra equipment were stored.

"The courts are acrylic," Russ said proudly. "And protected from the wind. Also, they face north–south so there's never any sun in the players' eyes."

"Have you ever considered putting in more courts?" Cynthia asked. "Look at all the people waiting to play. And it would be nice to have a snack bar out here to serve drinks to the players after their game."

"Yes, I've thought about doing that, someday," Russ admitted.

"An instruction center, with a hitting wall and ball machine would be a good idea, too," she said as Russ led her past the swimming pool to the main office building. Cynthia admired the lush grounds, such a beautiful contrast to the sparse desert surrounding them. "The *casitas*, as you call the guest rooms, are lovely," she said.

"And you've left room to put in another row of them right across here, so that they form a quadrangle around the pool. That would be nice," she mused.

"How clever of you to notice I left room for expansion in my original plans," Russ commented enthusastically. "Look over there, Cynthia. See the quail? We've got more wildlife and birds here than you would believe. People think of the desert as a barren place, but do you know there are almost 300 species of birds flying in and out of here? Whitewing doves, cardinals, orioles, mockingbirds. You never know what you might see."

They stepped onto a wide wooden veranda that ran around the main building on three sides. Bright yellow marigolds bloomed profusely in a flower bed alongside the porch, their pungent scent filling the air.

"Let's see," Cynthia said, taking a deep breath. "I've already seen the dining room. How about the lounge and front office?"

"Oh, I try to avoid the office if I can," Russ said with a lazy grin. "Every time I go in there the girls come running to me with a question to answer or something to do. As long as they can't find me, they get along just fine."

Cynthia could see that Russ enjoyed playing the part of the fun-loving host with nothing on his mind except good times. But she knew his careless attitude was just a cover. Merely seeing how smoothly the guest ranch operation ran, she knew he was doing a good job of managing it.

As they walked through the lounge, Cynthia admired the southwestern decor, in keeping with the adobe exterior of the building. On two sides of the room, large round-topped windows were set into the thick walls with wooden shutters painted a bright blue framing each side, ready to close out the hot sun when necessary. Long couches surrounded a huge whitewashed fireplace with tile trim, and game tables and shelves full of books filled the perimeter of the room, making it a pleasant place for guests to gather. One end of the room contained a wooden counter that served as a reservations desk and beyond that was the office.

With a reluctant sigh Russ led Cynthia into those back rooms. "Cynthia, meet Sonya," he said. "She's in charge of the dining room. Now, Sonya, do you have some delicious new recipe for me to taste-test today?"

"No, but can I complain to you about the price of tomatoes and beef and bakery goods?" she asked Russ with a harried smile, holding out some order forms she was filling in.

"Later, Sonya, later. See what I mean, Cynthia? They save up all their problems for me. Now meet Alice. She keeps our reservations unsnarled."

"And I have a dilly of a problem for you today, Russ Fielding," said the pink-cheeked redhead who's hair was straggling out of a haphazard pony tail. "I want to talk to you about Miss Betty Jo Blevins. This is the fourth day in a row she hasn't shown up for work. She hasn't even bothered to call in. When I tried to call her apartment house, the superintendent said he hasn't seen her."

Alice gestured toward a third desk in the office that was piled high with ledger books and trays of unprocessed paperwork.

Russ drew one hand through his windblown hair and down the back of his neck. "I guess we'll have to go ahead and replace her." Suddenly his eyes flared wide open with inspiration, and Cynthia knew at once what he meant by his questioning look.

Maybe it wasn't a bad idea. She moved over to the desk and began absently leafing through some of the papers strewn across it. She picked up an ashtray full of lipstick-stained cigarette stubs and emptied it into the waste basket.

"It may take us days to find a suitable person," Alice was complaining.

"We need someone to tell us in a hurry if we're making any money," Russ said. Cynthia felt his eyes on her. "Mr. Vickers will be coming out here for his quarterly report pretty soon," he added.

Cynthia sat down behind the empty desk and began gathering up scattered pencils and putting them neatly in a cup. She leafed through a stack of purchase orders and invoices that looked like they'd been ignored for weeks. There was a lot of work to do. Even when Betty Jo Blevins had been coming to the office, she'd obviously been doing a less than admirable job.

"We haven't prepared any profit-and-loss statements, there are no budgets, and we haven't done any banking since last Friday," Alice said.

"We certainly are in a mess," Russ

agreed with exaggerated self-pity. He walked over to stand beside Cynthia's desk.

She cleared a space on one corner of her desk, near the adding machine, which she noticed had almost run out of paper. She found a new roll in the top desk drawer and began inserting it expertly. The place needed organizing. If fiscal matters weren't handled correctly, a small business could go down the drain in a hurry. She thought of all Russ had worked so hard to build.

"Alice, Sonya, go into my office and sit down with a cup of coffee for our morning meeting. I think I've solved the problem," Russ said quietly.

Cynthia loved hard work, and there was certainly plenty of that right here. She also liked to feel needed. She'd always been willing to jump in and fill a void. Fate seemed to be helping her make a difficult decision.

Russ leaned close to her. "You're staying, aren't you?"

"Of course, I'm staying," she agreed, giving him a sparkling smile. She wasn't just referring to the pile of papers on the desk in front of her as she grinned back at her new boss and added, "How can I resist such a challenge!"

Chapter Three

"What are you going to wear on your date with Mr. Fielding?" Merry asked as she followed Cynthia into the room, her arms burdened with packages.

"I'm not going on a date," Cynthia replied. "He's just going to drive me around Tucson to show me some of the sights."

"But you said he mentioned something about dinner afterward at the Tack Room, and that's the best restaurant in town."

"That's his way of thanking me for getting his office straightened out. Now, let's see what we've got here."

She dumped her load of bulging bags and boxes onto the bed. The women had spent the whole morning at Goldwater's Department Store, outfitting Cynthia with jeans, boots, and homespun cottons. Now they were littering Cynthia's room in the employee's bunk house with debris as they unwrapped everything.

Just the day before, Cynthia had insisted

to Russ that she moved out of the beautiful guest *casita* so that it would be available for paying guests. Now she occupied an upstairs room right across the hall from Merry's. The two of them had become close friends when the Indian woman helped Cynthia move in.

"I wish we'd had more time to shop," Cynthia said. "I wanted to visit some of the stores that carry Indian crafts so that you could explain everything to me. What a shame our ranch guests don't have more access to such products. Wouldn't it be nice if we had an Indian crafts shop right here at the ranch?"

"Oh, what a wonderful idea, Cynthia! Do you think Mr. Fielding would agree to it? I know where to obtain kachina dolls and Navaho rugs, and, of course, the peridot jewelry of my own people."

"I'll talk to Russ about it tonight. If he builds that new wing of guest rooms, we could squeeze in a space right next to the dining room. You could be in charge of it."

"That would be wonderful." Merry's dark eyes shone with enthusiasm as she turned to watch Cynthia unwrap the next package. "That's the dress, the new black one! That's the one you must wear tonight

72

for Mr. Fielding. And I have the perfect belt to go with it." She ran across the hall to her room and came back insisting that Cynthia get dressed right away so that she could check the effect.

Cynthia took a quick shower, then modeled the dress for Merry. The knee-length skirt was full with a wide ruffle of the same light cotton fabric around the bottom. Cynthia wore a loose blouse over it. With the beautiful belt of Indian silver around her waist, the soft fabric billowed out to give Cynthia's slender figure the fullness it needed to make the style very flattering.

"I think I've turned you into more of an Indian maiden than I am," Merry said, laughing as she studied the effect.

With the hint of a burnished copper tan on her cheekbones from her afternoon walks in the sun, Cynthia looked healthier than ever. Her eyes no longer had the sunken, hollow appearance characteristic of someone who has been chronically ill. She wore her hair in a less complicated style now, too – straight with a slight curve under at the ends to round the angular planes of her thin face.

Even though she had been spending long

days at her desk, bringing financial order out of the chaos the former bookkeeper had left behind, Cynthia wasn't tired. The calm, unrushed atmosphere of the ranch office, which reflected Russ's personality, had already had a soothing effect on her. She was learning to pace herself, not to tense up over every minor crisis.

Walking at a relaxed easygoing pace, she met Russ at three o'clock in the main lounge. A familiar deep voice called out, "Well, don't you look the very picture of southwestern chic. I'd say your shopping trip was a big success." He gave a long wolf whistle as he led her outside to the ranch station wagon.

Instead of wearing jeans, his usual costume around the ranch, Russ had on a pair of well-cut slacks that accented the lean length of his legs. A silky long-sleeved shirt of pale yellow and a vest of tawny leather covered his chest, and he threw a sports coat into the back of the car just in case the night became cool. He'd wet-combed his usually sun-and-wind roughened hair so that he looked like a cowboy all spruced up for the Saturday night barn dance.

"It's about time you had an afternoon off

for good behavior," he told Cynthia as he started up the car. "You've been chained to that desk for more than a week."

"I love my job. It's been fun learning all the ins and outs of running a guest ranch."

"And you've learned it all, I suppose," Russ said, giving her a sparkling smile that made her feel giddy.

"Not yet, but I'm working on it. I have lots of questions to ask you."

"I refuse to mix business and pleasure, so there won't be any ranch talk today," Russ insisted. "Stop trying to take charge, Cynthia. Just let things run by themselves, that's what I do. You'd be surprised how well they work out."

Russ made everything seem so effortless, which was the most endearing part of his charm. Cynthia wished she could learn from him how to drop all thoughts of work and take time out just to enjoy herself.

"Oh, Russ," she laughed. "You pretend you couldn't care less about the success of the guest ranch, but I know you well enough to see through that act of yours. I saw your eyes light up when I mentioned adding on those new rooms and tennis courts. And wait until you hear about my idea for a gift shop."

"Cyn-thi-a!" Russ drew her name out into three long syllables and gave her a warning look that pitched his blond moustache at a rakish angle across his tanned face. "One more word about ranch business and I'm tossing you out of the car."

Cynthia had prepared a mental agenda for her afternoon with Russ, but now she ticked off all the items she would have to wait to have answered. She'd hoped to use this time alone with him to learn more about his plans for the ranch, but she forced herself to put those matters to the back of her mind and tried to concentrate instead on the beautiful land they were driving through.

"I thought we were going to tour Tucson. You've been heading out of town now for ten minutes," she said.

"I'm taking you to the Papago Indian Reservation, to a mountaintop so high they've put the world's most powerful telescope on top of it. From there I can show you everything at once."

"Oh, how exciting. Tell me all about the Papagos."

During the rest of the ride up to the nearly 7,000-foot Kitt Peak, Cynthia soaked up Indian lore as Russell told her exciting or amusing anecdotes passed along to him by Papago acquaintances he'd met at their annual rodeo in Sells. Once they stood on the viewing platform near the famous National Observatory, Cynthia felt as if she was on top of the world.

"That's Baboquivari Peak, jutting up there to the south," Russ pointed out. "It's a sacred place to the Indian people. To the north is Picacho Peak, near the state's only Civil War battleground."

"Why, the mountains are beautiful," Cynthia exclaimed.

"From here you can see all the way from our humble rancho in Tucson clear down to Mexico," Russ said, bending down to point over her shoulder and turning her in the direction he wanted her to look. "Some afternoon I'll run you down there to go shopping in Nogales and get some tamales at a little place I know of."

"It's all so magnificent, I'm speechless," Cynthia murmured.

Birds soared through the air – hawks, perhaps, or maybe even eagles. They took her breath away with their aerial stunts near the sheer, high granite ridge where she was standing.

Russ kept one arm draped casually over her shoulders, letting his broad hand fall almost to her breast. She reached up and took it absently in her fingers, fully absorbed in the striking desert vistas surrounding them on all sides. Not speaking, Russ stared intently down at her face, watching her drink in the beauty of the scene. His gaze communicated pride, as if he had created all this for her himself.

Finally he spoke in a cautious whisper, tugging at her two hands as he spoke. "If I can tear you away from all this, we have more to see."

The grandeur of the scenery around them had almost mesmerized Cynthia, but suddenly she realized with a start that she was still clinging to Russ's hand with both of hers. Her fingers began to tremble as she tried to accept this intimacy as naturally as he did. It meant nothing to him to put his arm around her. He'd done it since the first day they'd met. But now even his most innocent gesture seemed full of significance, and she made a conscious effort not to overreact to his physical closeness.

When she escaped his grip with a stiff, thrusting movement that she hoped didn't offend him, he quickly grabbed one of her hands again and held it loosely as they walked back to the car.

"Before it gets too late, I want to take you to the Arizona-Sonora Desert Museum," he told her. "I think you'll like the displays of native animals in their natural habitats. We can't see it all. There are twelve acres of movie sets, mines, petroglyphs, and saguaro forests, but we'll explore a little of it before the sun does down."

Much later, they made a last stop before dinner at a bright whitewashed building Cynthia had asked Russ about when she'd first seen its dramatic dome and spires from various points in Tucson. He explained that the Mission San Xavier del Bac was known as the White Dove of the Desert and was a beautifully restored example of the Spanish mission architecture of the 1700s. They went inside to admire the murals and the altar, and Cynthia discovered that the mission still served as the site of worship for the local Indian population.

Several Indian children brushed past them in the semi-darkness. Then, as they rounded a hallway corner just outside the main sanctuary, Cynthia noticed one small auburn-skinned boy crouched by himself, crying sadly.

"Oh, Russ, look at that sweet child!" she cried, kneeling beside the boy and reaching out to gently touch his hair. When he didn't pull away from her, she asked, "Are you lost? Are you looking for someone?" But the boy's blank stare made it clear he didn't understand. "Oh, I wish I knew some of the Indian languages. Someday Merry is going to teach me hers, but that won't help me now."

Cynthia stood the boy up, wiped the tears from his face, and spoke to him as calmly as if he could understand every word. "Now there is no reason to cry. I'm going to stay here with you until we find out where you're supposed to be. Don't be afraid, you're going to be all right. Oh, you are the sweetest thing," she crooned to him reassuringly.

Impulsively she leaned over and kissed his streaked cheek. To her surprise, she was instantly rewarded with a wide smile.

"He seems to understand your meaning if not your words," Russ said from just behind Cynthia, his voice so soft that she hardly recognized it.

Just then a teenage girl came running

80

around the corner, saw the boy and, with a shrug of relief, grabbed his hand and towed him off behind her in the direction she'd come from.

"Wasn't he a darling, Russ?" Cynthia asked with a rush of emotion. She could still feel the soft touch of the little Indian boy's hand on her arm. "I'd love to have a little boy like that. I used to wonder what a child of mine would look like. I used to..."

She stopped talking as she realized Russ was staring at her intently. "I'm surprised you and Chuck didn't have kids," he said quietly.

"We just kept putting it off," she replied lightly. Though her heart was hammering, her manner was as offhand as possible. "You know how that goes." She hurried back to the car. Strolling slowly along, Russ reached the vehicle several minutes after she did. She was waiting for him inside.

"I suppose you didn't want to give up your career just to raise children," Russ said as he got into the car.

She didn't answer, biting her lower lip to stop the flow of words that she would probably regret later if she began sharing

81

her feelings on the matter with him.

He seemed to sense from her lack of response that he was treading on a delicate personal matter. He leaned slowly back in his seat, stretching to squeeze his fingers into the pockets of his tight pants to extract the car keys.

As soon as he put the key into the ignition, the car radio leaped into a loud cacophony of guitar music. Rather than turn it down, he let it blare for a few moments, and Cynthia was glad he hadn't insisted they continue the discussion.

After a plaintive Willie Nelson tune died down, Russ turned the radio volume low. "We're going out Sabino Canyon Road to the Rancho Del Rio Tennis Club. I like to visit the competition now and then, and besides, the Tack Room is the best restaurant in Tucson. Someday I hope to build as good a restaurant at my place."

"He'd said "my place." Cynthia looked across at him, her surprise taking her mind off of her own internal musings for a moment. She'd never before heard him refer to Mr. Vickers' property as his own. Was he even aware of his proprietary interest in Haven Hills Tennis Ranch?

Russ reached across the car seat to take

her hand. "You'll like this restaurant. It's in a romantic spot, nestled right up against the foot of the Santa Catalina Mountains. It's a forty-year-old adobe hacienda with roaring fireplaces and cold margaritas."

With one thumb he was gently massaging the tender skin on the palm of Cynthia's hand. She stirred restlessly, realizing he was trying to lift her spirits. He must have noticed her lack of response to his plans for the evening. Seeing the little boy and remembering all of the disappointments of the last few years had spoiled her hopes for this time alone with Russ. She had wanted to test the waters today, explore her new feelings toward him. But instead, the haunting refrains of her old sorrows were interfering. Was there no way to escape the past and begin again? Cynthia felt an unbearable tightness across her forehead, and she closed her eyes for a moment.

"Russ, I have a headache," she finally said. "I hate to spoil the evening, but I wonder if I could have a rain check on that dinner."

He took his eyes off the road long enough to give her a concerned look, and she wondered if the compassion she read on his face meant that he understood the crazy emotional ups and downs she kept experiencing when she was with him.

"It's been a long day," he said, turning the car around. "I'm the one who keeps telling you to slow down and get more rest. I'll take you home if you want, but only if you promise to meet me for tennis tomorrow. I won't have you sneaking to the office to work on Sunday. I'll meet you at the courts at noon."

At high noon the next day the Arizona sky was the deepest blue Cynthia had ever seen. She walked to the tennis courts feeling rejuvenated by a good night's sleep, and eager to show Russ how quickly her spirits had recovered. The sun felt warm on her bare legs beneath the short white piqué tennis dress she wore with blue ruffled panties that peeked out from the hemline as she walked.

When she arrived at the courts and saw that they were, as usual, all full, she pulled Russ to a table apart from the others, insisting they wait until all the guests who wanted to play had gone in for lunch. "Let's sit and talk in the sun," she suggested.

Russ stretched out in a chair next to her so that one thigh rested indolently against hers. She accepted the casual intimacy for one delicious moment before moving her bare leg away from him as she considered the business questions she wanted to ask him.

"Now that I've had a chance to look over the account books in the office, I can see that you've made this ranch into a very profitable business for Mr. Vickers. He must be very grateful."

"I think he is," Russ acknowledged, his hands clasped in his lap. She noticed he never fidgeted with restless energy the way she did, but always seemed content to sit placidly wherever he was.

"But Mr. Vickers owns everything, doesn't he? I mean, you helped him plan and build this guest facility, but it's on property he owns and all the profits from the rental of the guest accommodations go to him."

"That's right. And I have a beautiful home to live in, which he let me build to my exact specifications. There's beer in the ice box, bread on the table, and I have pretty partners whenever I want to play."

He gestured toward the fluttering flock

of women dressed in white waiting to get on the courts, but Cynthia knew he meant more than tennis games.

"What have I got to complain about?' he asked her with a contented half-smile.

"Have you ever given thought to the future, to building up an equity in this place? Mr. Vickers is making all the money, building up a valuable asset, and you're doing all the work."

"This is work?" Russ asked with a teasing smile, reaching his arms lazily around him in a wide circle.

"What I mean is, wouldn't you like to own the ranch yourself someday?"

"I've never really thought about it."

"But you have. Last night you called it 'my place.' Remember?"

"By golly, aren't you sharp to have picked up on that?" he said, giving her a smile. Then he looked across the courts to the compound of tile-roofed buildings he had planned, seemingly deep in thought. "Maybe I have had kind of a secret hankering to own this."

"Have you ever talked to Mr. Vickers about it?"

"There's no way I could buy an expensive piece of property like this."

"But I think you should talk to Mr. Vickers. He wouldn't ask you for all the money up front. You could pay him off on a long-term mortgage."

"But then I'd have a big bill to meet every month."

"Russ, you could do it," Cynthia insisted. "I've studied the books."

"Do you think so?" he asked, looking as pleased as if she'd just presented him with a valuable gift. Then his face clouded. "Where did you get such an idea anyway, Cynthia? I don't need all that aggravation." He rose with a shrug of indifference and headed for the small building where the tennis office was located.

"I don't mean to be pushy," she said, following behind him. "Or to put ideas into your head that weren't there already." She hoped he didn't think she was stepping out of bounds with her suggestions. But she had studied the numbers carefully and was confident her plan could work and that Russ would want to know about it.

She followed him inside the cool, dark office, where all the shades were drawn against the hot midday sun. She was still apologizing when she noticed that Russ had stopped by the door and was closing it slowly behind her. A mischievous expression covered his face.

"Now that I've got you trapped in here alone with me," he said, "let's see how you are at arguing your point."

Cynthia looked around her with surprise, noticing that she was, indeed, enclosed in a room with only one door. And that door was being leaned against by over six feet of hulking, formidable masculinity clothed in very brief white shorts that revealed long muscles cording powerful brown legs. There was obviously no way to force past him. A bit nervous, she threw herself into the chair behind the cluttered desk, pretending to ignore Russ's aggressive stance.

"I can envision all the things you want to do around here," Cynthia chattered. "With adequate financing from a local bank you could build the tennis courts you need and add on a row of guest suites. Of course, if you were the owner, these would be your decisions."

Russ walked toward her. She tried to believe that the glint in his eye was only his usual frisky look of happiness. But his face had taken on a dark, determined look, as if he weren't listening to anything she was saying.

"And Merry and I have come up with a wonderful idea for a gift shop right here at the ranch that would feature Indian products," Cynthia continued, growing increasingly bewildered. Her heart was beating almost painfully in her breast.

"Plans, plans, plans," Russ murmured. "You're just full of ideas, aren't you, little darlin'? Well, I have some plans of my own."

"What do you mean?" she asked, alarmed, rising swiftly to her feet as she saw him slowly stalking her, still moving toward the desk.

"Back in the old days you used to give me lots of arguments on every subject," he said, following her evasive movements. "And I remember I had a wonderful idea of how to quiet that busy minds of yours, only I wasn't free to use it then."

"You mean when we used to know each other in college?" She was stalling for time.

"Yes. You were married then, and I was engaged to Helene." He was standing disturbingly close to her now, and as she backed away, closer to the wall of tennis rackets behind her, he kept moving inexorably forward. "It would hardly have been proper in those days to end our arguments like this."

"What do you mean *like this*? Trapping me in a little room, and then trying to intimidate me by looking fierce and – "

Cynthia's words were stilled as her lips came beneath the crushing dominance of Russ Fielding's. His kiss blanked out further speech and most of her rational thought, as well. Suddenly only feeling was left, but that was all that she needed. Tiny explosions ran all along the length of her body where he was pressing closer to her. And where his mouth covered hers with such exquisite mastery, she felt open and receptive, free of the cold emptiness of the last, unloving years of her life.

Her eyes squeezed tightly shut in ecstasy, she saw the pinks and vermilions of Arizona sunsets and the blazing heat of ranch bonfires. Heat seared her skin as blood rushed to her head and she released herself in a giddy swoon against Russ's chest.

Russ parted his legs in a more secure stance and pulled her small body into an even more enveloping embrace, her feet almost between his, her hips pressed into the warm curve of his tennis shorts. Her breasts felt the hardness of his chest with as much detail as if she were pressing her sensitive fingers there, for her whole body had become an erotic instrument, feeling pleasure from every throbbing nerve ending.

Russ pulled his mouth away from hers and mumbled with a hoarse chuckle against her ear, "Are you ready to concede the argument yet?" before moving his lips down her neck to her hot shoulders.

"Russ, I . . .' Cynthia found herself laughing, with an outpouring of delight at every bewitching touch of Russ's moustache down the sensitive slope of her neck beneath her brown hair.

"It's the moustache, isn't it? It's tickling you. Hush up, now, or you'll hurt my feelings."

She wanted to tell him she loved the way his searching upper lip felt against her skin, every exploratory motion it made intensified by the harsh brush of the moustache against her skin. But before she could say anything, he had pressed his lips over hers again to stifle her laugh into a eruption of giggles that vibrated their mouths against one another's in new and uniquely sensual ways, leading them both to more unbridled pursuit of the pleasures this kiss had to offer.

Russ's hands were now beneath her brief tennis dress, slipping impudently underneath the waistband of the ruffled shorts, which were all she was wearing beneath it. Slowly he eased down her backbone until his big hands grasped her rounded bare skin in two handfuls, pressing her pelvis into his to increase the bond between their slowly undulating bodies.

Cynthia's heart fluttered almost out of control with the rampant desire coursing through her. Her temples throbbed until she felt they might burst, and every nerve in her body screamed for the comfort of release. She rocked her hips against his, felt the promise of where the next moment would lead them, and opened her mouth invitingly beneath his. His instant surge of possession strengthened his hold on her.

Then, suddenly and unexpectedly, Cynthia's glorious rapture hung suspended in midair, stopped as if a bird in flight had been frozen onto a photographic plate. Time stood still as a primitive anxiety began its oppressive and sticky crawl upward across her emotions. Her heart was still beating rapidly, her lips still yearned for those that titillated hers. But she began to feel an inexplicable fear.

She pulled partly away from Russ's embrace, her body suddenly stiff, her eyes wide as she tried to remember who he was and why she was in his arms. The plesasant warmth at the back of her neck turned to a sudden chill.

"Let yourself go, Cynthia," Russ breathed softly near her cheek, not releasing her from his powerful grasp. "Can't you learn to relax and enjoy something totally?"

"No, I can't," she said, looking up into his face with a beseeching expression.

He took her cheeks between his broad hands, framing her pale face with his long brown fingers. "There's nothing to be afraid of. I merely want you to enjoy yourself, to express your feelings in the oldest and best way ever devised."

"You're rushing me," she said in halting words.

"Isn't five years long enough to wait for this?" he asked with a slight smile.

"I feel as if I only met you last week. I'm so confused! My body responds to you one way, and my mind is still trying to catch up. I have to change all my attitudes about you."

"I'll help speed things up just a little bit," he murmured, his blue eyes taking on the glow of the cloudless Arizona skies as he studied her. Now he began coaxing, trying with small kisses upon her fluttering eyelashes and her inflamed cheeks to reawaken the passion that he'd priefly glimpsed.

She gave a regretful sigh. "Please stop, Russ. Please try to understand. I've been through a year or two of hell. Men aren't high on my priority list."

"I'm not *men*, you know," he argued, giving the word a nasty emphasis she hoped hadn't been in her voice. 'This is your old buddy, Russ, who cares for you."

"Chuck once claimed he cared for me, too. And look what happened when I believed him," she said. "Trusting in love got me a six-year sentence. Six years of unhappiness."

"Give yourself a chance. You'll trust in love again," he said, caressing her cheeks lightly with his thumbs. His movements were so gentle and patient, so soothing, that she wondered briefly if he would continue for hours – or however long it took – to relight the fire that had burned so pleasantly for them a few moments before.

But Cynthia pulled away from him. His closeness now was torture, arousing as it did images of what those moments could have led to, the dangerous fire he was trying to draw her into, where she might tumble into the forgetfulness of desire. What if she fell in love with him? What if she commited herself to him, just as once before, she had commited herself to Chuck? If she trusted in love again, she might have to suffer the pains of watching it die.

If she were to remain here doing the work she loved, in this place she now loved, she must shield herself from Russ, protect herself from the detonating effect of his caresses. A cold sob of regret filled her throat, and she hurried across the room and ran outside, bravely trying to assure herself that she had self-control enough to resist his strong temptation. But one thing she knew now. Arizona was not the serene and peaceful place she'd hoped for.

Chapter Four

When Cynthia walked into the office the next morning, she had no time to worry about how to face Russ after her hurried escape from the tennis shack. Sonya was rushing toward the door to the kitchen as Cynthia came in. "I've got to get a pot of chili going. Mr. Vickers is coming today, and he always expects a bowl of my chili for lunch."

"Does that mean Mr. Vickers will want to go over the books with me?" Cynthia asked, quickly pushing away the routine paperwork on her desk to sit down in front of the big green ledger books that she hoped were up to date.

"That's usually the most important part of his visit," Sonya said. "He's a real business wizard. He can see things in those numbers that no one else can."

Cynthia's hands fluttered nervously over the pages of her entries, hoping she'd double-checked carefully enough. "If only Russ had warned me about this. If I had just one more day," Cynthia mumbled as Sonya hurried out the door.

"One more day for what?" Russ asked, having approached her desk so quietly that she hadn't been aware of his presence.

"To get my figures ready for Mr. Vickers. You never told me he was coming for a meeting today."

"I didn't know myself until his secretary called this morning. And if you had another day to get ready, you'd just spend it fretting and worrying."

Cynthia turned to give him a quick smile. "You know me so well." She sighed and he pulled up a chair from Alice's empty desk and straddled it to sit facing Cynthia, watching her bustling activity.

"You have the account books in better order than they've ever been, now stop worrying. We've got all the information we need."

"All the information we need for what?"

"I'm going to talk to Max today about buying Haven Hills Tennis Ranch."

"Oh, Russ, I'm so glad you've decided to try it!"

"I think the idea's been in the back of my mind for a long time. But are you sure I can afford it?"

"The numbers don't lie," Cynthia replied confidently. "What made you change your mind? You didn't seem convinced yesterday."

Russ got up and began pacing in front of her, clapping his hands in front and in back of him, obviously excited about his plan.

"I keep remembering what it was like five years ago when this place was under construction. I was excited and happy then, always busy, always anticipating what I'd do next. But since then I've gotten lazy. You're right about those additions we need, but I haven't been motivated enough to get them done."

"But if this was your own ranch, you'd get things done."

"Yep. I just need a little of your famous drive to inspire me to action, I guess." His face glowed like bright sunlight.

She looked up to study his face. He was leaning on his elbows, looking at her as if her determination amused him.

Something about Russ was different this morning. His face seemed younger, more open, and his skin shone as if he'd just returned from his habitual early-morning gallop. She wondered if the new hint of vulnerability in his face, however slight, meant that he had been as deeply affected by their ardent embrace yesterday as she had been. Perhaps he didn't know how to react to her now, either. She wondered if they could ever again behave naturally in each other's presence. Maybe if they lost themselves in work, if he bought the ranch property and began expanding it, they would both be so busy working together on the new projects that they could ignore their personal attraction and be close coworkers, nothing more. But as Cynthia studied his blue eyes, she wasn't at all sure that work would be distraction enough from his seductive powers.

"Well, at least I have a little time before Mr. Vickers gets here to put my papers in order," she said to break the growing tension between them.

Just then the door to the lounge burst open and Alice called into the room, "Mr. Vickers is here. I see his car pulling up out front. Guess he wants to get an early start this morning."

"Gosh darn it," Russ said. "I can't meet him right now. I have tennis lessons scheduled for those pretty little debutants from San Francisco."

"Oh, Russ, don't leave me alone with

him," Cynthia protested.

At that moment a portly man with a briefcase charged into the room and immediately asked to meet the replacement for the former bookkeeper. As Cynthia introduced herself, he threw down his wide-brimmed hat on one desk and removed his coat, which he draped around one of the secretarial chairs nearby.

"Let's take these things into the office where we can spread them out on Russell's desk," Max Vickers said.

He grabbed the monthly profit-and-loss statement Cynthia was tentatively holding out toward him, and she scurried to gather up whatever else they'd need as he headed into Russ's office.

Russ followed him. "Max, I have a couple of lessons I can't cancel. I'll have to talk with you a little later over lunch.'

'Can't stay today, my boy, even for that famous chili. Got meetings stacked up all day long."

"Well, then, I'll leave Cynthia here to do my dirty work for me," Russ said, ignoring the pleading look she was giving him. "I'm sure she can explain everything. Don't forget, Cynthia, to try out that purchase idea on Max. See what he thinks of it." He gave her a mischievous smile.

Cynthia narrowed her eyes and mouthed a silent retort, but Russ only tossed his head back with an unworried laugh of farewell and disappeared out the door. Apparently he felt more confident in her abilities than she did, for he seemed willing, if not relieved, to put the ranch-purchase proposal in her hands. Perhaps he felt an objective stranger could fight for the idea more effectively with his old friend that he could. But Cynthia was nervous at the thought of meeting alone with this business genius, Mr. Maxwell Vickers, Helene's father.

However, the meeting went quite well. Cynthia was able to answer every question the man asked, had every number he needed somewhere near her fast-moving fingertips.

"Little lady, for a brand-new book-keeper you've done a remarkable job catching up. I've never had so much information available to me before," he said, adjusting his wide girth in the chair as he leaned back and lit a long cigar.

"Mr. Vickers, I wonder if you'd do me a return favor and answer a few questions for me," she asked as she snapped shut her account book.

He looked surprised. "Why, of course. What do you want to know? You seem to have a pretty good grasp of how things are run around here."

"I was wondering if you ever considered computerizing all of this accounting. I worked in an office in Chicago where we installed an excellent data system."

"What does Russell think?"

"He's afraid our guests will object to getting a printout instead of a handwritten bill. Last week we got into quite an argument about it. I can't seem to convince him that a computer would free our time so that we could give the guests more personal attention than ever."

Vickers took a puff on his cigar and released the smoke slowly with a satisfied sigh. "You've got a good point there. Is this the matter Russ asked you to talk over with me?"

"Well, no," she admitted hesitantly, fidgeting with the buttons on her red-checked blouse.

"Then let's hear what's really on your mind," Max Vickers commanded.

"Actually, Mr. Vickers," she began, "it has to do with something Russ has been thinking about for a long time. I'm sure you're fully aware of how much time and energy and dedication Russ has put into the ranch. Well, he's begun to think a little more about the future, and well ... what it comes down to is that Russ would like to buy the ranch from you."

Max Vickers sat bolt upright in his chair, his wide face crinkling into a network of fine wrinkles, his shrewd eyes narrowing with speculation. He was clearly not pleased by Cynthia's suggestion. But, undaunted, she went on.

"If you'd give Russ a mortgage on the guest ranch and some of the acreage around it, he could pay it off to you in monthly installments out of the profits the ranch is making. I've checked all the figures for him. It can be done. And those profits would increase, I'm sure, if he felt he was his own boss, making his own decisions."

"If it's possible to increase the profits around here so easily, why should I sell the place?" Vickers asked her, his eyes now closed to mere slits, giving him a wily but inscrutable look.

"You'd be making a good profit on your investment. And I think you'd feel very good to reward the man who made it all possible. Russ has poured a lot of himself into this place. Just think of how proud he'd be to call himself the owner here instead of the manager."

"What makes you think Russell wants to take on a mortgage like that, with all the risk it involves? Seems to me he's happy just the way he is. Things are very easy for him right now."

"Maybe too easy. A little risk brings out the best in a businessman. He could turn this ranch into something very special if he owned it."

Max Vickers rose laboriously from the chair, his breathing heavy as he studied her carefully. "You're a spunky little lady. I have a daughter just about your age, and I wish she had just a bit more of your drive. You've made a convincing argument. But the answer is no."

Cynthia's disappointment drained the color from her face.

Vickers stubbed out his cigar in an ashtray and went on speaking from the gray cloud of smoke that enveloped him. "Russ is very important to me, and I wouldn't want to change that relationship, I like the feeling of having him around, almost part of the family."

Cynthia's eyes flared wide with new insight. Did the old man still hope that his daughter and Russ would get married someday? Russ had mentioned that he liked to be available for Helene when she came home on her intermittent visits. Perhaps Max Vickers thought that one day, when she tired of globe-trotting and decided to settle down, she'd find Russ an unofficial member of the family and agree to marry him.

"Russ is the kind of man who would always remain your friend, no matter how your business arrangement changed," Cynthia assured Mr. Vickers.

"You seem to think you know Russ pretty well," Vickers remarked as he stepped closer to her, suddenly appearing to take a more personal interest in her. "You aren't just some new little bookkeeper hired from a newspaper ad, are you? You said you've known Russ a long time?"

The old man's eyes were astute and probing in his fleshy face. "I went to college with Russ and Helene, too," Cynthia explained. "We were at Denver University together."

"Well, well, well. If you're a friend of

Helene's, then I'm sure you'll want to get on into town and see her real soon," the man said as if to subtly question her closeness to his daughter.

"I haven't called her yet because I heard she was out of town."

"I see. I see. Well, she's returning soon and I'm sure she'll high-tail it right out here to see *you*," Vickers said, still looking at Cynthia in that cagey cross-examiner's way. "My daughter always looks forward to coming to the ranch. That's another reason I intend to retain my interest in the place. It gives her a secure feeling to be out here with Russ."

To Cynthia he sounded as if he were referring to a mere schoolgirl who needed careful protection rather than a grown woman who thought nothing of traveling far distances alone.

"Sorry to shoot down this idea you've cooked up with Russ," Vickers said as he began preparing to leave. "As I say, I admire your outspokenness."

He waved cheerfully in farewell as he went out the door, as if to indicate that he didn't mind an occasional business tussle – and, perhaps, enjoyed it. Especially if he wound up on the winning side, firmly in control.

Cynthia threw herself behind her desk with a groan, realizing that she'd have to spend the entire afternoon and evening at her desk catching up on the work she hadn't gotten to because of the long morning meeting and her futile discussion with Mr. Vickers.

At five o'clock, when Alice finished work and went home, Cynthia left the office, too. She took a stroll about the grounds, hoping to meet Merry for their customary glass of iced tea before she had to return to her desk for another hour or so of work before dinner.

She headed across the lawn near the swimming pool, looking for the laundry cart that Merry pushed around as she cleaned rooms. Instead she saw a well-bronzed form rise from a lounge chair beside the pool and stretch his long arms into the air, as if awakening after a long nap.

Silhouetted against the darkening sky of late afternoon, Russ's body looked magnificent. There was little hair upon his broad chest, nothing to hide the awesome details of his well-developed muscles. His skin, smooth and sun-tanned to perfection, without a ripple or a pale spot, seemed to cover him like thick, creamy butterscotch sauce over a sundae. He was wearing slightly damp white canvas swimming trunks, indicating he'd been in for a dip. But, despite the considerable impact of his tautly handsome physique stretched out before Cynthia's bemused gaze, his face drew her most rapt attention.

"Now I know what's different about you!" she exclaimed.

Russ looked over at her walking toward him from the grass at the edge of the paving, his sleepy eyes staring back at her with the dazed look of someone who's been napping.

"You've shaved off your moustache. Your moustache is gone."

He rubbed both hands across his smooth face, as if he couldn't really remember if what she had said were true. The gesture seemed to wake him up, and he gave her a slow, seductive smile.

"I aim to please my lady friends, Cynthia," he said. "And that giggle I heard yesterday during my most ardent lovemaking convinced me I had to make some changes if I wanted to please you."

She blushed at the way he easily

discussed what to her had been a very anxiety-provoking incident.

He started to lean down to pick up a towel, and she gasped almost audibly at the sight of his tight stomach muscles contracting in an intricate pattern across his midsection. Her own waist pulled inward with empty longing.

He was wrapping the towel around himself sarong fashion to cover the wet trunks. "I'm going inside to get us a couple of beers. Stay here and wait for me."

"No, I have to get back and—"

"That was not an invitation, it was an order. I'm the boss and you're the employee, remember? I want to talk to you, so wait here." He nudged her gently into a lounge chair.

She couldn't help turning all the way around to watch him stride across the grass. Her eyes fastened with interest on the double rounds of his backside undulating beneath the soft fold of the towel as he walked with languid grace and a subtle thrust of his pelvis.

Several female hotel guests called out, "Hello, Mr. Fielding!" hoping to attract his attention, before he returned to Cynthia with the beer.

"What did you want to talk to me about?" she asked.

"I'm mad as hell at you."

"You are?" She almost choked on her first sip of ice-cold beer. "You don't *look* mad. You don't *sound* mad." She studied him carefully, convinced that he seemed as placid as ever.

"I don't waste my time getting all riled up. But I'm good and mad at you, just the same. Why, after Max Vickers called me this afternoon, I had to come out here and swim forty laps of the pool."

Now she began to suspect what had angered him and was doubly impressed that he could appear so calm and restrained. But his well-controlled rage was almost more agonizing to face than if he'd blustered and shouted at her. She twisted uncomfortably in her chair.

"You had me smoking pipe dreams, honey," Russ accused her. "I don't know why I listened to you about buying this ranch. Max Vickers told me he'll never sell."

"I'm sorry you're disappointed."

"I was very happy with things just the way they were until you started inspiring me with these big ideas of yours. I can see

110

now how you exhausted Chuck if you were pushing at him that way all the time."

"Oh, how dare you say that, Russell Fielding!" she cried out angrily. "We already settled that one before." Where did he get such ideas? she fumed.

The pool area was deserted, so no guests were within hearing distance and both of them could feel free to unleash their pent-up anger.

"You probably thought you could pressure Chuck into getting ahead in the world faster than he wanted to," Russ told her, "but that won't work on me."

She stood up unsteadily on legs that suddenly seemed incapable of supporting her. A tornado of emotions raged within her. "Chuck Price was the most unscrupulous, the most deceitful, the most cruelly ambitious man I've ever known. How dare you accuse me of pushing *him*!"

"Now simmer down, Cynthia," Russ said, leaning back to take a long draught of beer, refusing to become caught up in her anger. He tipped his head back to drink several swallows of beer in a row, and her fury increased in the face of such casual opposition.

"You don't know what he made me do!"

she cried. "You don't understand what he did to our lives just so he could move up the corporate ladder faster than the guy at the next desk. He took me to live in Chicago, where I was constantly sick. He forced me to work at whatever jobs I could get in order to finance a new car and a country club membership. And he made me go on working, even when ... even when I wanted to quit. He was making plenty of money. But he insisted that we needed enough to buy a house in a better part of town, to impress his bosses. He wouldn't let me quit my job. No matter what. And there's more." She stopped, out of breath, afraid she'd said too much already.

The thought of what lengths Chuck had gone to in order to keep their two incomes rolling in made Cynthia feel so weak that all her anger disappeared, and she sank into her chair again, completely defeated.

"Here, drink this." Russ was holding her glass of beer out toward her as a gesture of reconciliation. "I'm sorry. I didn't realize what bitter memories I would uncover."

Cynthia took one sip and held the foamy brown liquid in her mouth for just a second, enjoying the soothing coolness before she quickly swallowed it. When she was more composed she went on, choosing her words carefully, trying to make Russ understand.

"Sure, I'll admit I was a college girl with big dreams for the future. And I guess I married Chuck because he seemed to be as motivated as I was, anxious to take on the whole world. We were attracted to each other because we were alike, and we had good times when we were still in school, talking about what we were going to do. But, when I found out what he was willing to do in order to achieve that success, to what lengths he was willing to go, I was shocked. Nothing in the world is worth betraying your moral principles."

"What did Chuck do?" Russ asked gently.

"He lied to people. He would do or say whatever was necessary in order to get what he wanted. I watched him do it year after year until I lost all respect for him. But it hurt more when I discovered he was treating me the same traitorous way he treated his coworkers. That was the end." She wiped one hand across her face to clear away the tear or two that had squeezed out of her eyes. "Excuse me, I've got to get back to work," she said, starting to get up.

"No, you're upset, and you're not going back to work tonight," Russ said firmly. He drained the last of his beer and stood up, then pulled her to her feet. "I'm going to walk you to your room, and you're going to get some rest before you come to the dining room for one of Sonya's famous roast beef dinners. Afterward, there's going to be square dancing in the lounge, and I want you to be my partner."

"No, Russ, I don't feel like it, really."

Russ draped an arm across her shoulders and led her toward the employee bunk house as if she had no will of her own. Her outburst had left her beyond caring what happened next.

"I'm the one who was angry, and now look at this," Russ said. "I'm the one doing all the making up. Just how did you pull that little trick on me, lady?" He smiled down at her, and Cynthia noticed the expansion of that patch of pale skin of his upper lip where the moustache had been, almost missing it. It cheered her to remember it tickling her shoulders, making her shudder and shiver with delight. But Russ looked younger now, more gentle and forgiving.

"I'm sorry for building up your hopes about buying the ranch," she said as they ducked beneath an overhanging tree branch and started along the path behind the pool.

Russ gave her a swift sideways glance. "Oh, I guess it doesn't hurt to reach for the stars now and then. This idea may work yet. We'll just let Max think about it for a while. He could change his mind." Russ was smiling slightly.

"Why, you shifty-eyed, cattle-stealing mother of a jackass," she cried out with mock ferocity, drawing away from him and glaring at him.

Russ laughed uproariously. "You should see yourself when you're angry," he said. "Lightning shoots out of those smoky eyes of yours, and your face lights up like a pinball machine."

"Well, I have good reason to be mad! Here you gave me such a reprimand and made me feel so guilty, and now I find out for sure that buying the ranch is something you want and hope for just as much as I do. Besides, you suggested I broach the subject with Vickers."

"I guess it's just become a habit to fight with you," he said. "I kind of enjoy it, as a

115

matter of fact." He leaned down to whisper in her ear, as if it were a secret he wanted no one else to hear. "You see, making up after a good brawl is the best part."

All at once he began singing, his voice wavering in gutteral but evocative tones. "I'm just going to love making up with you you you." Cynthia couldn't help laughing.

As Cynthia started up the stairs of the bunk house, Russ came with her, placing one hand lightly on her back and then inching it up her spine teasingly to bring it to rest beneath her hair, on the warm skin at the nape of her neck.

"After today you'll look forward to an occasional fight with me," he said in a husky tone. "I'm going to show you how much fun it can be to kiss and make up."

"What do you mean??"

"What do you think I mean?" he teased, and Cynthia froze, her footsteps poised between treds on the stairway. "I'm coming upstairs with you."

Her pulse beat madly. "Please, don't. I thought I explained to you yesterday. I'm not ready for this. I'm afraid of you." His words had thrown her into frightened confusion.

Russ stopped, too, one foot on the step

above them so that the towel around his waist split open, revealing his brown legs and the seductive cling of his white swimming trunks.

"You're not afraid of me," he said. "You're just plain afraid. Afraid to let yourself go. But I'm going to teach you to love those wildfire emotions you're holding back."

"It's much more than that, Russ," she said, letting him pull her gently toward him. "I did let myself love someone once, and I was betrayed. I can't forget that."

Russ pulled her within his arms up the last few steps to the door of her room, then leaned back against her door and pulled her even closer. Her hands went flat against his chest in protest, then the fingers slowly curled into a more compliant pose as she felt the soothing solace of being close to Russ.

He tried to kiss her, but she dodged her head away. When he bobbed his neck to chase after her lips, she finally submitted to him, but she felt none of the exhilaration of the last time he'd kissed her. One of his hands went to the nape of her neck, and the other curled possessively around her waist.

"The way you fear my kiss tells me more

117

about your marriage than anything you could say. What's happened to you? What did he do to you?" Russ asked, his eyes as blue as a mountain stream as he looked down at her, trying to share her pain, probe her dark secret.

Cynthia shook her head, unable to speak, aware of his fingers moving with slow sensuousness along the side of her neck. He was awakening her feelings again with his sympathy, with his careful caresses. She felt her gnawing fear give way to an even more awesome feeling. The first hot licking flames of sexual appetite began leaping up within her. Her secret cravings were slowly unleashed as the hand he'd placed around her waist moved under her blouse and began exploring sensitive places she made no effort to forbid to him.

"Russ, I don't want to be afraid. I want to feel alive again." She groaned against his bare chest, her lips moving against his hot skin as she kissed him.

"That's all I wanted to hear. If you're willing to try, to trust me, then there's nothing to worry about. Just leave everything to me."

"Oh, Russ..." she said, throwing her head back to protest, but the rising tide within her made the words catch in her throat, and she replaced them with a tremulous sigh of acquiescence. Her knees grew weak, barely able to support her, and she could think of nothing but the leisurely path of Russ's fingers across her quivering breasts.

Feelings that had been so slow to emerge the last time he'd held her in his arms, in the hot little shack beside the tennis courts, now came coursing through her body in a heedless rush that she knew could not be stilled even by her most damning fears.

He reached behind himself to open the door, and willingly she let him draw her inside the room. But just then footsteps came pounding up the stairway.

"Mr. Fielding? Are you up here?" Cynthia recognized the voice of the night clerk.

Immediately she drew away from Russell, surprised to find the front of her blouse unbuttoned to the waist, and her breasts, which she rarely confined within a bra, exposed to Russ's ravenous gaze.

He gave a slow coughing sound, then called, "Yes, Tim?"

"There's a call for you, Mr. Fielding," Tim called, his voice closer, "and it must be important. It's long distance from New York. It's Miss Helene Vickers, and she says she wants to talk to you because she's coming home. She'll be here tomorrow afternoon." The young boy's voice from outside the room sounded high pitched with excitement, as if it were a thrill for him to announce the expected return of someone so special.

Russ never gave Cynthia another look. Whatever passionate pursuit had heated his emotions just a moment before now seemed forgotten. "I'll come right now and take the call," he said and followed the boy down the stairs, leaving Cynthia feeling suddenly bereft.

Just when she'd gathered the nerve to make the plunge off the high dive, the water had been drained from the pool and she was left wavering high atop a dangerously gaping pit, her body taut with expectation, her nerves atingle with thoughts of the daring act she had been ready to attempt. But there was nothing left for her to do but climb quietly down the ladder alone.

Chapter Five

Cynthia dressed with care the next morning, slowly pulling on a pair of jeans and an especially flattering blue T-shirt. Then for the first time she put on the cowboy boots of chocolate brown suede that Merry had insisted she buy because they almost exactly matched the color of her hair. The traditional tall heels of the boots added a few inches to her height and made her feel more ready to face the day and Helene's arrival at Haven Hills. Cynthia noticed with surprise that the pounds she'd added since eating Sonya's heavy ranch house cooking looked good on her, filling out the curves of her buttocks and thighs.

As she brushed her hair, she looked out her window across the emerald rectangle of lawn and spotted Russ heading for the office, earlier than usual and with a purposeful stride. She stood transfixed, watching him with every nerve alert as she tried to sense his mood this morning. She could almost feel his keyed-up attitude, almost sense the tension of his hurried pace. Were his thoughts on Helene's return? Cynthia felt a stab of jealousy that alarmed her because of its intensity.

After Russ disappeared from her view, she sat down on the bed. With a flash of self-awareness she realized why these odd tuggings of jealousy were dampening her usually high spirits. She wanted Russ for her very own. She wanted to be part of his thoughts. She wanted to be the face he carried in his mind. She wanted to be the one he sought out to satisfy his needs. He had become more than an old friend to her, even more than a handsome single man whose touch enflamed her senses. She was in love with him, more completely in love than she'd ever been before.

She wanted to run his ranch with him, eat her meals with him, sleep in his bed with him, share all his thoughts with him, and never be separated from him again. She wanted to be important to him, as important as he was to her. Just the sight of him out her window could fill her with feelings of unfulfilled love and yearning.

Her breath catching in her throat, she hurried down the stairs. Already it might be too late. For now that Helene was back, Cynthia and Russ would have little opportunity to explore their feelings for each other. How could she be certain if he had room in his life for her, or if Helene still had a claim on his love?

When Cynthia got to the office, Russ was behind his desk, processing paperwork so fast that his OUT box was already overflowing. Usually he greeted each of his employees with an exuberant welcome as they arrived for work, and sometimes a hug if they were close enough. But today he barely lifted his head to speak.

"The man from the computer company wants to come by later today," Cynthia said timidly at his office door.

"Set it up any time next week," he said without emotion, his hand going to his head to rake through his sun-lightened hair, leaving it thoroughly disheveled, like loosely bundled hay, across his forehead.

"Here's a bowl of that new chowder recipe for you to try," Sonya said, entering Russ's office sometime later.

"Not at ten o'clock in the morning, if you don't mind." He dismissed her absently.

When the head wrangler came in to share

his latest dirty joke with Russ and got only a mild response, every one in the office accepted the fact that Russ was in an unusually preoccupied mood, and by mutual agreement they left him alone until lunchtime.

Cynthia was the only one still there when he stuck his head out of his office door to check the clock for what seemed like the hundredth time. He gave another big sigh. "Want to walk over to the dining room with me for lunch?" he asked. "On the way we can fight over whether or not we need that computer."

"Sure," Cynthia hastened to agree, hoping that one of their favorite controversies would keep his mind off of waiting for Helene.

They crossed the cantina area and were almost at the steps of the dining hall when they heard the sound of delighted, high-pitched laughter and the buzz of many voices coming from inside.

"Helene's here," Russ said, stopping dead in his tracks.

Before they could proceed inside, the double doors burst open and Helene rushed outside to greet them.

"Russell darling! I'm home!" she

squealed, throwing herself into his arms.

Cynthia would have known Helene anywhere, dressed as she was in a fluffy, ruffled dress of pale peach so like the ultrafeminine styles she had worn in college. She had gained weight since then, but it was not unattractive. She had always had a round, cheerful face, only now there seemed a bit more flesh to the jawline, a touch of extra fullness to the cheeks. Where once she'd worn her hair in gentle curls, she now sported one of the new permanent waves, and the effect was charmingly disheveled.

"And our old chum, Cynthia!" Helene cried, catching sight of her. "Daddy told me you were here on a visit." She looked Cynthia over from top to bottom curiously, as if to judge just how harshly the years had treated her.

Helene kept one hand intimately around Russ's neck, and Cynthia watched with fascination as her long red nails twined themselves through the hair at the base of his neck, where it hung over the collar of his plaid shirt, too long and in need of cutting but apparently too inviting for Helene to resist caressing.

"When Daddy called me last night he

said I should hurry on home and welcome my old college friend. If I'd known you were coming," she continued, addressing Cynthia, "of course I would have left New York sooner and arranged to be here to greet you." Helene smiled.

"I wrote to you," Cynthia began. "Well, I mean I wrote to both of you here at the ranch. You see, there was a mix-up. I thought you lived here, that you and Russ were married and running the ranch together. You never wrote and told me otherwise, you know. And that's why I didn't hesitate to come out here to stay with you and recuperate."

"And now we can have great fun together, getting reacquainted," Helene said. "Come on inside, Russ. I have a surprise for you. I want you to meet Jean Claude Rabaix."

"Who exactly is he?" Russ asked, reaching up to take her hand away from the back of his neck and then holding it lovingly in his. Cynthia watched the movement until she saw that Russ had noticed her staring. She turned hastily away, her face reddening.

"I've brought us the most wonderful French chef from New York City," Helene bubbled on. "I've convinced him to come here and help Sonya plan some really elegant continental menus."

"You mean you've brought your new friend here to work at the ranch?" Russ asked, a note of coolness in his voice that seemed to indicate he was capable of jealousy. He dropped Helene's hand.

"Yes, run in and greet him, Russ, will you, and introduce him to his new coworkers. I think he's feeling a little displaced right now."

Russ disappeared inside without another word, and Cynthia stood dumbfounded, marveling at the way Helene could institute such a major change at the ranch with so little opposition, while Russ often rejected out of hand her own more sensible suggestions.

"Bring us a wine cooler by the pool, will you darling?" Helene called out to a waiter who was hurrying by. "Come on, Cindy. Let's sit down here for a moment and catch up on all the news."

"How was New York?" Cynthia asked.

"Oh, that was only a stopover. I've just spent five months in France. I had the most exciting time. I fell madly in love with an art student. We rode in a hot-air balloon

127

over the vineyards of Bordeaux and lived in a garret in Montmartre. We sat in cafés every evening drinking wine. It was so romantic."

Helene sounded like a breathless college girl. In fact, her vision of the idyllic days in Paris reminded Cynthia of every young woman's fantasy of a summer fling.

"It must have been hard to leave there," she commented.

Helene's enthusiastic smile vanished. "Oh, things didn't work out. They never do. But I have Russ to come home to, no matter how far my adventures take me. It feels so good to be home." She stretched her pale arms up to the sun.

Cynthia had the eerie sensation that she was continuing a conversation of five years ago with Helene. In the intervening time, Russ had established a guest ranch, and Cynthia had married, divorced, and developed her business talents. Even Chuck had grown in some ways. At least he had refined his ability to social climb. But, to Cynthia's surprise, she realized Helene had remained unchanged. She seemed frozen in that fun-loving post-adolescent state that was so appealing in college girls but seemed vapid and shallow in a woman who should be getting on with life.

"And what have you been up to?" Helene asked.

"My life hasn't been nearly as exciting as yours, I'm sure." Cynthia said. "I never adjusted to the Chicago weather. I was sick constantly with bronchitis. And I worked hard, all the time. I worked at my job and I worked at my marriage. But in the end it wasn't enough. I wrote to you about it."

"You *did* leave Chuck? You walked away from that darling guy?" Helene exclaimed, her softly rounded cheeks pink with consternation.

"I haven't just left him. I divorced him. It's all very final, Helene, so there's no point in berating me about it. I've done all that myself, long ago."

"Well, I just can't believe it. Chuck was such fun. You'll have a hard time finding another man like him."

"I'm not looking for another man."

"Oh?" Helene asked, accepting a tall drink from the waiter, who had hurried to carry out her order. "I'd have guessed husband-hunting had brought you out here to cowboy country."

Cynthia wondered if Helene thought she'd come here to start up a romance with

Russ. Helene had always been very possessive about him, and Cynthia guessed that was one of the many things about her that hadn't changed much since college days.

"I came here to recover my health," she said. "I wanted to visit you both. When I found Russ was here alone, my first reaction was to leave."

"Oh, really?" Helene inquired.

"Russ and I are right back at our usual pattern of fighting and arguing all the time. Remember how we used to get going on politics?" Cynthia asked with forced lightness, hoping to convince Helene – and herself – that she and Russ were an unlikely romantic couple.

But Helene refused to join in Cynthia's amusing reminiscences, or to agree to the humorous incompatibility of Russ and Cynthia. She picked up her glass without saying a word and took several hasty swallows.

"Russ and I can't agree on anything, even now," Cynthia chatted on as Helene watched her over the rim of her almost empty glass. "We take different sides on every issue that comes up."

"Opposites attract," Helene commented

tersely, no discernible expression on her face.

"Oh no, not in this case," Cynthia hurried to say.

"Did Russell explain to you why we never got married?" Helene asked her suddenly.

"Not really. He just said something came up at the last minute and that the next day you canceled all the wedding plans."

"Yes, I did," Helene said. "I wasn't ready to be tied to some overcritical bully, and Russ can be that way sometimes, for all his country-casual pretenses, you know. I needed more time to be single and enjoy life, but I'll be ready to settle down with Russ someday. Maybe it will be this year. My father would like that," she said, her eyes squinted as if she were already picturing the elaborate wedding festivities.

Cynthia had learned to be wary of Helene during that last year at college when they had played tennis and double dated, always at Helene's instigation. She'd noticed how Helene manipulated her friends, encouraging Russ to spend time with Chuck and Cynthia, who were newly married and seemed very happy. Then she'd heard the fanciful talk of the guest ranch Helene and Russ planned to build someday in Arizona. Helene got Russ so intrigued with making plans that before long Cynthia was staring at Helene's victorious face as Russ announced their June Wedding. Helene had used Chuck and Cynthia to help her get Russ. She was an expert at getting what she wanted.

As strong as her newly realized feelings for Russ were, Cynthia did not want to fight Helene for Russ's attentions. Helene hadn't changed. The years had in no way matured her. And Cynthia knew she would be an awesome opponent if she felt ready to marry Russ, as she was saying, or even if she merely wanted to retain him as her available refuge to fly back to between her romantic adventures abroad.

Cynthia noticed Russ heading toward them from across the lawn. At the sight of his jaunty step her heart quickened its beat. She wanted to jump up and throw herself into his arms with as much confidence as Helene had earlier. But Cynthia didn't dare present such a direct challenge to Helene, especially when she wasn't sure about Russ's true feelings.

"Russ, I've just had a wonderful idea," Helene said, reaching out to grab his hand when he came to stand beside her chair. She massaged it lightly as she spoke. "I'm going to have Jean Claude cook up a special treat for tomorrow night in the dining room. A banquet for all the guests and some of the staff, too. It will be a welcome for Cynthia, in honor of her visit to Arizona. And, of course, we'll celebrate my return, as well. There'll be champagne and toasts and speeches. Oh, won't it be fun? Something different instead of that usual dreary Friday night chuck-wagon dinner."

"Oh, but we can't tomorrow night, Russ," Cynthia blurted out without thinking. Helene, apparently shocked that Cynthia would voice any opposition to her plan, turned to give her a wide-eyed stare.

"Friday nights Cynthia and I have a regular meeting set up at my house to go over the paperwork I can't face at the office," Russ explained, taking up a position right behind Helene's chair and putting both hands on her shoulders as if to try to physically impose a mood of acceptance.

"Cynthia works here?" Helene asked slowly, obviously surprised.

"She came along just at the right time to replace Betty Jo. Wasn't that lucky?"

"Lucky, yes," Helene mused with an interested and more alert expression. "And you have this regular Friday night habit that can't be broken, is that it? Some sort of business meeting that precludes your coming to my party?"

"I'm afraid so," Russ said, thrusting his hands in his jeans pockets, looking disappointed.

Actually Cynthia was surprised that Russ was sticking to his commitment so resolutely. They'd struck this bargain only a few days before. Russ had promised her that, without exception, she could talk to him every Friday evening about whatever office problems they hadn't had time to settle during the week. She in turn had agreed to hold the meetings in a pleasant atmosphere during supper on his quiet patio. She had to admire Russ for rejecting the temptation that Helene had unwittingly dangled in front of him for fun instead of work. It would've been easy, she was sure, to postpone this first Friday night dinner meeting to attend the banquet Helene was planning.

"Well," Helene said, looking significantly from one to the other. "The French party is going right ahead without you two. If you're too busy to welcome Jean Claude properly by letting him show what he can do, then I'll do it alone."

"Whatever you want," Russ agreed with a sigh of resignation. "Just check all this out with Sonya. She probably has the Friday night preparations underway already."

"I'll tell her to cancel those plans and turn her kitchen over to Jean Claude at once," Helene said with a light trill of laughter that indicated her enthusiasm for her new project. "Shall we go in to lunch?" she asked, standing up to loop her hand through Russ's arm. The two of them walked off across the grass while Cynthia fell in place behind them, apparently forgotten by them both.

Her heart twisted as she watched Russ bend his fair head close to Helene's shoulder as they exchanged whispered confidences, their steps in perfect unison as they strolled together at an unhurried pace. How good they looked together, just as they always had. The golden boy and his unworried, always-smiling companion. Forever young, forever happy, they might have stepped out of the pages of a fairy tale.

Cynthia experienced the wrenching

sorrow of hopelessness as she wondered once again if she'd come to love Russ too late. After too many wasted years, too many opportunities missed, it was bad timing to fall in love with him now and expect him to give up longstanding relationships and return her own passionate feelings.

But that evening, as she dressed to meet him, her optimism revived slightly. After all, he had chosen to spend the evening with her. He had stood up to Helene's beguiling plans. It was encouraging to consider that she might have won a preliminary round already without even realizing it. Tonight alone with him she would be able to assess his feelings at last. Tonight she would know if she truly was capable of winning his heart.

She had time for only a quick shower, and then she slipped on a simple long dress of crinkly cotton. It was bright yellow, the color of a desert sunrise, and trimmed with a wide band of matching Mexican lace at the square neckline. Because she would be climbing the steep path to the house, she wore flat sandals, which added to the peasant effect of the dress. She was heartened by the sight of herself in the mirror. Her more robust figure and healthy suntan, which made her face look as nut brown as a native Indian's between the curtains of straight, clean brown hair, were proof that she had put all the grieving of the past behind her. Arizona was working its miracle cure on her already, and falling in love had served as a potent remedy, as well.

As she left her room she carried under her arm a manila envelope stuffed full of papers to go over with Russ. The grounds were deserted, and she could hear boisterous voices coming from the dining room, where the party had already begun. She loved Haven Hills at this time of night, when the guests were all so happily taken care of inside and she had the desert vistas to herself.

As she climbed the hill, she stopped several times to catch her breath and to watch the first glimmer of a star here and there in the darkening sky. The Catalina Mountains still held the glow of a magnificent desert sunset, a spectacle that each evening at dusk left the land in a fiery bath of color for a breathless hour.

"Are you ever going to make it up the hill?" Russ called to her from his doorway.

She had stopped to gaze at the distant foothills.

"Yes, I'm all right. You're the one who's always telling me to take the time to smell the flowers. That's what I'm doing, enjoying the beautiful evening."

"Well, that's a good sign. I guess we've finally slowed you down to our country pace."

Cynthia crossed the tile parking area in front of the house as Russell stood watching her, holding the massive door open for her.

"Now, if you'd forgotten to bring along that envelope of papers, I'd be sure your recovery was complete," he said with a smile, taking the paperwork from her hand as she walked past him and throwing it across the room to the coffee table.

"Give that back to me, Russ!" she said hotly. "I want to show you a construction estimate I've gotten for you on that addition."

"How about a drink before we get to work? Is that all right with you, slave driver?" he asked with a slow smile. His hair was still damp from his shower, comb marks still showing in the dark blond hair that would soon dry into lighter shades and a looser arrangement. He was wearing a long-sleeved cotton shirt that was unbuttoned halfway down his chest. His feet were bare, which made Cynthia wonder if she'd arrived early.

"Do you want to finish dressing first?" she asked.

Russ's laughter rang through the room. "I'll have you know I consider myself perfectly dressed for an evening at home. If you can come up here in your nightgown, I guess I can spend the evening without any shoes on."

"This is not a nightgown..." she started to explain, but he had disappeared into the kitchen. He returned moments later with two margaritas in giant-sized stemmed glasses rimmed with salt.

"I made these good and big so I won't have to interrupt our discussions to get refills. Aren't you impressed by my businesslike attitude?"

"I'm impressed that you chose this boring meeting when you could have gone to a fancy party."

"No discussion with you is boring, Cynthia," he said with a crooked grin. "Actually, your enthusiasm is so darn catching I'm enjoying my work more than I have in a long time. Now, what are we going to hash over tonight?"

Cynthia took her drink and sat down on the sofa. She spread out the contents of the envelope she'd brought. "I went ahead and got a rough estimate of what it would cost to add on that wing of rooms and the new tennis courts. If you and Mr. Vickers decide to go ahead with the project, of course," she added.

"Aren't you the busy one! Why did you do that?"

"I know how disappointed you were when Mr. Vickers vetoed my suggestion that you buy the ranch. So I thought you might like to look ahead to another project."

"Your old theory of frantic activity as a universal cure-all? Well, it might do the trick," he admitted, a bright blue sparkle of humor in his eyes.

"Just because Mr. Vickers turned down the sales proposal doesn't mean he'll turn down remodeling plans," she explained.

"Tell me honestly." He took the piece of paper she had offered him and gave it a dubious look. "Is it essential that we add these facilities? Can I convince Max of that?"

"Look at this projection I've prepared. If

there were more guest rooms, the profit margin would change completely. With the same staff, the same – ”

“You haven’t tried your drink yet.”

“Oh, yes. Mmmm. That’s good. While I drink, you look over those numbers.”

Russ gave her a teasing look. “I wonder if I could supervise all this construction and still get in my daily horseback ride and swim.”

“Oh, you’d manage, I’m sure of that.” She smiled. “Now that I have the bookkeeping all organized, I’ll have more time to take some other responsibilities off of your shoulders. If you want me to.”

“Of course I want you to.” Their gazes locked and held. Finally Russ stood up and reached for her hand.

“Let’s move outside. I’m barbecuing chicken tonight and it has to be turned over every ten minutes.”

They sat down at the outdoor table, sipping their drinks and eating tortilla chips dipped in a hot red sauce. The sky slowly grew darker until the lights of the ranch stood out below them like a relief map for their inspection. But from way up in Russ’s hideaway, the ranch seemed far away and unreal to Cynthia, and the

141

problems she'd brought with her seemed unimportant. Here she felt isolated from all those practical, everyday problems. Making the most of their valuable time alone together was what seemed of primary importance right now. Their discussion quickly ran out of steam, forgotten by both of them in the balmy glow of the warm evening.

Cynthia had another drink with Russ while he finished cooking the chicken, and then she tossed another of her cut-lettuce salads. She kicked off her sandals and came to sit with her bare feet close to Russ's beneath the table, which was now lit by a candle in a hurricane-glass holder.

Russ had brushed a thick red barbecue sauce over the chicken, and Cynthia could feel the sweet, sticky sauce all over her fingers and the corners of her mouth as she devoured piece after piece of the succulent meat. To her surprise, Russ eventually excused himself and brought her a steaming scented towel with which to wipe her face and hands.

"You've certainly convinced me you liked that chicken." He laughed, gazing at her sauce-smeared lips.

"How did you manage to stay so clean?"

she demanded to know.

"I ate mine with a knife and fork," he said, pretending to brag, but his eyes danced merrily at the possibility of a new controversy between them.

"You sound as if you think I'm not capable of such superior abilities. I happen to prefer eating chicken with my hands."

Russ wiped her fingers for her. "You cut lettuce with a knive and eat chicken with your hands. You do everything wrong," he said, shaking his head.

"It happens to be completely proper to eat chicken that way, according to all the rules of etiquette," she said, defending herself very seriously, as if the argument mattered.

He took the small towel and gently dabbed it across her nose and lips. "There you are, as clean and kissable as ever," he said with an unmistakable huskiness.

"How do you do that, get the towel so hot and so fragrant?" she asked, trying to keep a light tone. He was crouching before her, and she found that her hands were resting quite naturally on his knees.

"It's an old Oriental trick. Only I do it in the microwave oven." He laughed.

"You've perfumed this with your

cologne, haven't you?" she said, taking the towel from him and burying her face in her favorite lemony smell.

"I didn't think you'd noticed what cologne I use," he said in a low voice. "Now that you're clean and decent, come and curl up with me over here and let's count stars for awhile and tell each other how wonderful we are."

He took her hand and pulled her from the chair before she could complain, then led her to the cushioned chaise lounge at the far edge of the patio. The curved canvas top over one end of the couchlike chair made it look like a miniature covered wagon, and it had ample room for two.

Cynthia was so relaxed by the slow and easy pace of the evening that, before she knew it, she was snuggled within the circle of Russ's arms as they lay side by side on the chaise. She hadn't expected the evening to take such an intimate turn, but she put up no protest.

"So you really want to put me to work on this expansion project?" Russ whispered near her ear, so softly that his breath felt like an evening breeze descending from the foothills of the nearby Catalina range, dimly outlined in the darkness in front of them.

"Yes. I think it's important for the success of the ranch."

"And success means a lot to you, doesn't it?"

"Is that so bad? What do you have against ambition?"

"I tease you for some of your big plans, and I'm sorry about that," he said gently. Then his manner became playful. "But you must excuse my ornery ways, cuz you know I really do burn and lust after you, little darlin'," he said, imitating an unskilled actor in a western movie. "I only aim to please you, ma'am." His accent had become more cowpoke than college graduate, and she couldn't help laughing.

Russ hugged her closer to him as he went on in a normal voice. "It's hard to resist you, Cynthia. You just never give up. And when I have you close to me like this, I feel like you could get me fired up to do almost anything."

She looked up into his face, but it was too dark to tell just how serious he was. "You'd be willing to do anything?" she asked.

"Yes, anything. Especially if you asked me to kiss you."

Cynthia didn't have to ask. Russ bent to the task as accommodatingly as if it was all her idea, and he was determined to give her more than she'd bargained for.

The sweetness of his kiss was familiar to her now, and as welcome as a warm shower on a cold night. All the day's tension and stiffness floated away, and she curled against the long, hard length of him, as if she knew that her proper place was in his arms. When he drew his lips away from hers, he held her just as close as ever, and she felt his heart booming through the thin fabric of her dress, beating in perfect time to her own heart. She stared at him, astonished at how close she felt to him.

Flashes of reflected light shone in his eyes as he kept his face close to hers, as if he were searching for clues to her feelings in her expression. His chest rose and fell evenly and his breath was warm on her cheek. She let the minutes tick by. Perfectly gratified, she enjoyed the peace of being close to another person, trusting and satisfied.

She reached up with one lazy finger and began to stroke the side of his face, and he gave a husky groan in response that sent shivers of delight down her spine. She

146

moved her searching finger across his sensitive upper lip, now so smoothly enticing, an inviting gateway to the mouth that could please her so. She stroked the length of his sun-tanned nose, straight and well shaped, and gave a flippant little brush to each of his eyelids, where the lashes feathered across his high cheekbones. His eyes were closed, his head thrown back in obvious pleasure.

Cynthia slowly stretched her arms over her head, then lowered them onto Russell's shoulders. She was enjoying this uninhibited moment of pleasure with the man she loved, with no thought of what might follow.

Somewhere far away music was playing, guitars were strumming in a rocking waltz that loosened and blew away every last care in Cynthia's world. She was melting, feeling so heavy on the couch that nothing could move her; she was an extension of Russ's body and could never again function separately from him. He would simply have to drag her along with him wherever he decided to go.

Russell was humming to the music. He had turned on some tapes when they were inside the house, but now an errant shift in the evening breezes brought the sounds out to their ears. Cynthia felt the comforting rumble within his chest as he crooned to her softly, wordless, throaty sounds that gave precise messages of building desire.

After many happy minutes had passed, Russell's hands began moving over her hips and thighs, steadily in time to the music, until he had drifted her dress up above her knees. All she had worn beneath the dress was the tiniest bikini underpants, and before long she could feel strong, insistent hands upon the silky fabric, tugging at it as playfully as a puppy with a new toy. He made low growling noises that brought a smile to her lips.

"I want you to stay here with me tonight," Russ said thickly, close to her ear. Before she could respond he was kissing her.

This time he brought a pulsing passion to the kiss that took her by surprise. His tongue darted between her teeth in short, stabbing explorations, then circled sensuously within her moist mouth, revealing delicious secrets with every movement, promising her the further feelings he could unleash within her when she was willing.

Later she couldn't remember the precise moment when the explosion occurred within her, but it was sometime between Russ's impertinent suggestion that she stay with him and the moment when his lips left hers to begin their feverish journey down her body. Like the firing of a space rocket, with the same burning intensity, her body came alive with the shuddering full-scaled heat of arousal. She gave an exultant moan as she writhed within his arms, begging him for the rapture she knew he could bring her. She pulled off her dress as if her body was desperate for freedom, flinging it over her head as she heard the welcome sounds of Russell's clothing being stripped away.

At that moment she felt that her union with Russell was almost predetermined. Nothing could stop it. Cynthia's temples were pounding as the secret feelings of attraction she'd once tried so unsuccessfully to deny finally took glorious flight.

Molten-hot fire swept upward through every vein in her body and into every throbbing place that pulsed out her need for him. For just an instant, a flash of anxiety paralyzed her, and then her passion overrode her doubts, buried them in an avalanche of desire for Russell Fielding's love. She was swept into the ecstatic oblivion she craved.

Afterward Cynthia lay tenderly cradled in Russ's arms, reveling in the intense afterglow of their love-making, still warm despite the cool desert air on her naked body. The fire pit burned down to a circle of gray ash as the night turned colder. Finally Russ picked Cynthia up and carried her inside to his bedroom, where he made love to her again.

This time his water bed began a rhythmic accompaniment to their movements. The peaceful sway increased in intensity, matching the exciting tempo of Russ's pelvic thrusts. Then slowly it ebbed to quiet stillness, and Cynthia's pulse also grew still. Finally she fell asleep.

Chapter Six

Later, much later, as the dark night outside turned to rosy dawn, Cynthia opened her eyes and found herself lying across her lover's sprawled body. Languidly she reviewed every thrilling moment of his possession. Now she could rejoice in the sensations he'd so generously offered her; now she could muse on the delightful possibility that he'd given them to her out of love. For she had received and returned his outpouring of passion in an expression of her own heightened love for him. A love that grew more sure and strong with each passing moment.

The watery mattress beneath her moved, lulling her with its soothing motions as she rolled over onto her back, stretching voluptuously, fulfilled and content. She knew Russ was awake now, too, because every once in a while his hand moved slowly across her upper arm or sought a resting place on a bare breast that protruded casually from beneath the stiff white sheets. But neither of them spoke. They only uttered occasional sighs of contentment as they lounged together comfortably intertwined.

As light began to fill the room, Russ rolled over in a tangle of bedcovers and brushed her ear with taunting lips. 'I told you I hankered to do anything in the world to please you," he said huskily.

"And please me you did," she said, closing her eyes and curling up as close to him as possible.

"But you can have more, much more," he said after a slow yawn. "You can have my favorite tennis racket, my car, my Dolly Parton record collection. You name it."

"You're just sex dazed! You'll regret all this later," she warned him.

"You've got me where you want me, darlin'," he insisted. "I'm hog-tied and all yours. You can even have those new tennis courts and guest rooms. Build a whole damn convention center, if that's what you want. Ask me for anything!"

She thought of asking him for a declaration of love, for the promise of a permanent relationship. She would even settle for his assurance that he loved her right now or had loved her last night.

She sighed as she gently tangled her fingers in the hair on his forehead and brushed it out of his eyes. He must have noticed her slight melancholia that put an unwelcome shadow across their ideal morning.

"Stay still, princess. I'm going to squeeze you some juice right off my favorite grapefruit tree. I'll bring you the morning paper and a pitcher of French 75s, and then we're going to settle down right here. I'm going to show you how to enjoy a dandy Saturday morning. The fun is just beginning,' he yodeled as he leaped out of bed. She watched with wonder as his beautifully naked body disappeared through the bedroom door.

Russ was gone a long time. She heard the shower running, heard him banging around in the kitchen, but she felt no similar surge of energy. She was physically drained, unable to rise off of the bed. She turned over on her stomach and stretched crosswise across the wide water bed, relishing every inch of the space. She experimented with tapping one foot and rolled her hips slightly, trying the various jiggling effects the water bed could give as a smile of contentment formed on her lips, which were pressed into the warm sheets where Russ had so recently been sleeping.

When Russ finally returned, he had pulled on the same pajama bottoms she'd caught him in the first night she'd arrived in Tucson.

"Sit up, my lady. Your drink is ready."

"What exactly is a French 75?" she asked dubiously as he poured something that looked like plain grapefruit juice into a tall glass filled with ice.

"Oh, there's lots of juice in it. Plus a little champagne, vodka, brandy—lots of flavorings like that."

"Oh, Russ! I'll never get out of bed!" she laughed with delight.

"That's the idea." He smiled back at her, his face as bright and cheerful as the warm sun.

Cynthia sat up and looked around in vain for her clothes, finally wrapping herself modestly in the sheet. She took the glass he offered with one hand while brushing her tangled hair from her eyes with the other.

"You're being awfully good to me," she said, searching his gaze.

"Just my little way of saying thank you, ma'am. Thank you for giving me a glimpse of the real you last night." His voice grew more serious. "I've known you for a long time, Cynthia, but for the first time I've seen through that efficient exterior of yours and seen the soft and vulnerable person you really are. Why, you just open up like a flower at the touch of love."

Cynthia stared back at him, forgetting the drink in her hand. "I should be thanking *you*. You've turned my life around completely, Russ. You made me trust you enough to make love with you. I wasn't sure I could ever trust a man again.'

"How did Charles Price do that to you?"

"I don't want to talk about my ex-husband."

"We have to sometime," Russ insisted. "I want to get him out of here! Until last night, I felt as if he was a third person standing between us all the time. It was getting too crowded. Sometimes when you looked at me I was afraid you were seeing Chuck. Please tell me everything, honey. I want to know what he did to make you so distrustful."

He looked at her so tenderly, his eyes so warm, his voice so sincere, that she suddenly *wanted* to tell him all about Chuck.

"Until I met Chuck," she began, "I

thought I could believe someone who said he loved me, who made me promises."

"And Chuck lied to you."

"Chuck denied me the one thing I ever asked of him. The thing I wanted most in the world. After he'd promised it to me for so long!"

"What was the wish he wouldn't grant?"

"All I wanted was a child." She was surprised to find how easy it was to be completely frank and open with him.

"You wanted to have a baby? That's what he refused to give you? Hell, you should have come here to me years ago!" Russ gave a hard laugh, and she responded with a smile to let him know she appreciated his efforts to lighten her serious confession.

He sat down beside her and with easy grace placed one hand upon her hip, where it made a low rise beneath the sheet next to him. "Tell me the whole story," he encouraged her.

"That summer before we started our senior year of college, when he convinced me we should get married, he told me we would put off having children until we finished school, maybe even until he had gotten established in his career. Of course,

156

I saw the sense in that and agreed. But after we left school and moved to Chicago and he got a good job, I kept asking him if this was time to begin our family. He always insisted that I go on working, that we needed my salary so that we could live in the expensive lifestyle he wanted. Finally last year he admitted that he never wanted children. They would only interfere with his life. He needed to concentrate all his energies on getting ahead. He'd never planned on having children, he said. He'd only made those promises to keep me quiet. You see, Chuck had no time to love children, or to love his wife. Those things didn't matter to him."

"Before you married him, did he ever indicate that he didn't want children?" Russ asked gently.

"Of course not. I could never have married such a person."

Russ stood up and went to the wall of draperies across one end of his room and pulled them open so that a panorama of desert grays and greens filled the room. He stood looking out without speaking for a long time, then whirled around and stared at her.

"If you'd been my wife and wanted a

baby, I'd have gotten you pregnant on our honeymoon! I wouldn't have wasted a minute. You would have four or five little ones by now."

Cynthia's composure was shattered. She took a sip of the drink and found it cold and bittersweet, just like her feelings at that moment. "Chuck Price didn't feel that way about it," she said in a choked voice. "And so there were no children. As soon as I realized he'd lied to me, just as he lied to everyone else, our marriage began to disintegrate faster and faster. Finally I filed for divorce."

"So by the time you got here you were pretty convinced that men couldn't be trusted."

She looked up at him, thinking of the one simple promise she wanted to hear from his lips. If he'd only say he loved her, she would believe it. She knew now that he was different, that his word was good. If he would only give that one word! But an awkward silence fell between them.

"I'm not asking you for any promises," she said. "Maybe that's what I've learned from everything I've been through."

"I told you, Cynthia, that there's not much I could deny you this morning. So be careful what you ask for. Right now your eyes are saying something." He reached over and took the glass from her hand and put it on the table beside the bed. "Let's see now, what could it be? A love ballad sung for you alone?" With one hand he gently smoothed her hair away from one ear, then placed his lips close to her face. But instead of humming one of his favorite cowboy tunes, he kissed her on her ear lobe, and then moved to the nape of her neck, where he nuzzled her hair aside to reach her most sensitive, silky skin and kiss her with lingering softness.

"A kiss or two to start the day, is that what you're asking for?" he whispered. His hands had found their way beneath the sheet, where he was making long, stroking movements down the length of her body. Finally he threw the covering off of her, and his exploring fingers came to rest on her breasts. She gasped as all the remembered excitement of the night before came flooding back to life again. His touch was strong enough to stimulate yet light enough to tantalize as he wrapped his long fingers over her soft flesh, enfolding her breasts as carefully as if they were roses in full bloom and bending to kiss them just as admiringly. His thumbs fondled her rosy nipples with a rhythmic, circular motion as he lifted his head to stare into her eyes. Her lips parted with an involuntary shudder of joy as she prepared to receive his kiss.

Just then the phone rang, but Russ gave it no notice. His lips moved closer to hers. The bright glow of his blue eyes disappeared beneath his lowered lids, and he tapped her lips briefly, just once, with a light kiss.

"Too late to unplug the thing, I guess," he muttered as he sat up, leaning on one hand wedged between her neck and shoulder, tangled in her brown hair.

"Hello? Oh, Helene, good morning," he said into the phone, clearing his throat. "Yes ... yes ... yes, I see. ... Well, we certainly don't want Sonya getting upset about how her kitchen is being run. Of course I want to hear about the banquet. I'll be right down and you can tell me the whole story."

He hung up the phone and sprang off the bed to begin rummaging through the drawers of the oak dresser across the room. "I have to go," he said.

"Orders from headquarters?" Cynthia asked.

"Yes, duty calls. And sometimes at the most inopportune times."

"I thought that was Helene."

"It was. It seems there's a giant snafu in the kitchen, thanks to her darling Jean Claude, and she wants me to get down there and straighten things out."

"I see." Cynthia pulled the sheet around her again, noticing that, as he'd looked over at her to speak, the sight of her nude body, still curled with anticipation where he'd left her, had evoked no response in him.

"In case I forgot to tell you, you won a lot more than my heart last night," he said as he pulled a T-shirt over his head. Feeling a wrenching sense of loss, she watched as he rolled it down over his smooth brown chest, reminding her of a theatrical curtain closing in the middle of the third act.

"You convinced me about the additions we need around this place," he said as he zipped up his jeans. "I'm going to take that estimate over and show it to Max. I think I can win his approval. He's usually in favor of anything that could increase the profit margin. Then he can take it to his banker next week and line up our financing."

"Good," she said dispiritedly.

"I told you, you're a woman I can't say

no to," he said with a wink as he started for the door.

"What if I ask you to stay here with me now?" she asked in a small voice.

"You know I can't do that," he said, waving. "But keep the kettle on the fire, I'll be back." He blew her a kiss before disappearing.

Cynthia waited until she heard the thump of the front door slamming shut, then got up and went in search of the shower. True enough, she thought to herself, she'd won a victory last night in proving to him that the additions to the ranch were a good idea. But she'd obviously lost the war. For after promising her a lazy Saturday, her ardent lover had rushed from the bedroom at the first call from his former fiancée. After telling her he would grant her any wish, he ignored her request that he stay with her and hurried off to help Helene.

Cynthia felt the hollow – the old pain – of being betrayed by false promises. She stood under the shower for a long time, but the stinging water could not revive the blissful mood she'd felt upon waking just an hour earlier.

In the weeks that followed Cynthia remained as disillusioned as on the morning Russell had abandoned her. She had little opportunity for private contact with him, for he was busy with meetings away from the ranch, setting in motion the remodeling plans, which Mr. Vickers had enthusiastically approved. Contrary to what Cynthia had previously heard, Helene seemed very interested in spending time at the ranch and kept Russ busy with her demands during his leisure hours.

The following Friday night Sonya asked to join Russ and Cynthia's weekly dinner meeting. She served them a late supper of quiche and salad in the dining hall, and when the meal was over they discussed at length her grievances over the way the kitchen was now being run by the new French cook. When Sonya had left, somewhat mollified, Russ and Cynthia remained at a corner table in the deserted dining hall, finishing off their dessert.

"I haven't seen much of you lately," Russ said with what appeared to be an untroubled smile. Apparently he felt no guilt over his neglect of Cynthia.

She swirled the ice cream around in her dish, watching it melt like an iceberg in a cold sea of blueberry sauce. "I know you've been busier than usual," she said, keeping her head down so she wouldn't have to look up into his cool and distant eyes.

"You're the one who got me into all this, remember? I've been over to see Max several times, to meet with the contractor he's lined up."

"And to see Helene?" Cynthia asked, deciding it was time to get that subject out in the open.

"Yes. She seems quite interested in this project. She's even planning a party at her house for all the local media people and travel writers, to make an official announcement of the expansion plans. I don't know what's gotten into her. She's never paid this much attention to the ranch before. She's spending a lot of time here."

"Maybe because I'm here she feels she has to stay close to protect her interests."

"You think she sees you as some kind of threat to her?" Russ asked, a look of disbelief on his face.

"She depends on you, Russ. She told me she likes to have you to come home to between her trips. She may wonder if we've become more than old friends." She gave him a meaningful look, trying to convey

164

without asking that she herself was wondering about that very point.

"I *have* noticed a difference in her on this visit," he said, staring into shadows of the big room. Cynthia realized he had missed her subtle attempt to probe his feelings about their own relationship, and was concentrating instead on what Helene might be thinking.

"She does seem more high strung, as if she's under some sort of pressure. Maybe you're right, maybe she's worried about losing me. I know how she counts on my being here, but I never realized how much of my time and attention she requires. I've just slowly grown used to buoying her up."

At that moment Cynthia felt in need of his attention, but with a discouraged shake of her head she realized she wasn't going to get it. Perhaps Russ's lovemaking, which had meant so much to her, had just been his casual, friendly way of expressing affection. Maybe to him it was just a pleasant way to pass the time with someone he enjoyed.

He certainly didn't appear as preoccupied as Cynthia was with the necessity of clarifying their relationship. She had to assume he was totally unaware of the depth of her commitment, which, for her, their night together had solidified. If he had any inkling of the love she felt for him, surely he would be as concerned about her feelings right now as he was about Helene's.

Russ stood up, glancing at his watch. "Speaking of Helene, I'd better get over to the lounge. She asked me to meet some architect she brought to dinner. Oh, she said she'd be calling you about invitation lists and other details for this party of hers," he added over his shoulder as he left Cynthia, feeling lonely and betrayed, sitting in the empty dining hall.

The next day Helene called Cynthia several times. Cynthia had already taken on a great deal of extra work in order to free Russ's time for the remodeling. Now, with the party to organize as well, her day was a busy one.

At five o'clock the office was empty except for the night clerk, who had just reported for duty, and Cynthia, who had settled in for several hours more work. Suddenly a welcome face appeared at the doorway behind the front desk.

"Merry! I haven't had time for a coffee

break with you in ages," Cynthia cried.

"I know. And I bet you never even left your desk at lunch time."

"Sonya brought me a barbecued-beef sandwich. Say, I'm glad you stopped in. I want you to look over this floor plan for the gift shop and make sure the architect included enough storage space."

"Oh no you don't. No more business today. You come with me right now." Merry reached out to take Cynthia's hand and pull her from behind her desk. "The stores at the El Con Mall are open tonight. We're going shopping again. It was such fun last time."

"But I don't need a thing," Cynthia protested.

"Oh yes you do. I just heard Miss Vickers at the cantina having a drink with one of the guests and going on and on about the beautiful gown she's having made for the party she's giving in her home. You'll be going to that party, too, and you need a very special dress."

Merry dragged Cynthia from store to store in the modern El Conquistadores Mall, rejecting several dresses that Cynthia found more than adequate. But at last Cynthia tried one on to which Merry gave a grave nod of her head. The dress was made of gray-green jersey with sophisticated dolman sleeves and a long bias-cut skirt that molded itself like a second skin to Cynthia's newly rounded hips. Merry promised her a necklace of lime-green peridots made by her artisan uncle to wear with it.

As they drove back to their rooms at the ranch, they passed the stable area where Cynthia noticed a glow of light filling the night sky.

"That's the weekly bonfire," Merry explained. "Haven't you ever gone to it? It's great fun."

Now Cynthia could see that a guitarist was performing for a crowd of guests who were seated on stone benches around the fire pit.

Merry stopped the car. "I'll put your new dress in your room. You go on over and listen to the music for a while."

But just as Cynthia approached the group, everyone began getting up to leave.

"You came a little late for the festivities, didn't you?" Russ called out to her from somewhere amidst the people who were filing past in the dark.

"I went into town with Merry and just

got back," she explained. "I'm sorry to have missed the show. I understand Hank plays a mean guitar."

Russ made his way over to her. "Well, you just sit yourself down right here," he ordered, putting his arm around her shoulders and pulling her closer to the fire.

"See you later over at the cantina, Mr. Fielding," one of the departing guests called.

"I'll be right along, Mr. Wright. I owe you a drink for that marvelous story you told me," and he laughed again with obvious pleasure. Now that she was closer to the fire, Cynthia could see Russ more clearly, his head thrown back to reveal his white teeth. "Hank, get that guitar right back out of its case," he ordered. "I want you to give a special private concert for this hard-working employee of mine."

"Sure thing, Mr. Fielding," said the tall, thin man in a cowboy hat.

"Oh, Russ, that's not necessary," Cynthia protested. "I can come next week and hear – "

"Nonsense. You sit down here next to me and listen up to some fine music. How about 'Sweet Music Man,' Hank? And then, 'Loving Never Hurt Nobody,' and

'You Feel Good All Over,' and maybe that one Merle Haggard sings, 'Today I Started Loving You Again.'"

"Russ, you'll keep Hank here all night with these requests."

"I think he's my very best audience, ma'am," Hank said, returning his guitar as he anchored one foot up on the low brick wall around the fire pit.

"This is one of the perquisites of my job, and I intend to enjoy it," Russ said. "If I have to work so hard for a living, then I might as well take advantage of my own personal troubadour to play love songs for my pretty lady."

"Russ, I'm sorry you're having to work so hard lately. I – "

"Hush now and just listen to this music. Office hours are over. Enjoy, honey. Haven't I taught you that yet?"

He crossed one polished leather boot over the other, his legs stretched out for what seemed to be miles in front of him, and laced his fingers together behind his neck as he leaned back to enjoy the twangy country music Cynthia knew he loved.

The smile on his face was beatific, and she couldn't help wondering if she'd been able to inspire such an expression during their rapturous moments together. The thought of the most passionate of those moments created an uneasy stirring deep within her, and she moved about restlessly on the stone bench. Now that Russ had reawakened her erotic nature, she was constantly disturbed by tantalizing thoughts of what he had done to please her. Her yearning for more of his lovely ministrations had become an obsession with her. Her imagination ran wild, picturing the romantic settings where they might make love again, and the wonderful things he would teach her to do to thrill him as much as he thrilled her. She pictured in detail sensuous love scenes beside the swimming pool or even here in front of the fire.

"That fire light is making your face look absolutely devilish," Russ whispered in her ear as the first song ended.

She jumped, startled by the sound of his voice, afraid he could see her fantasies in the hot, bright sparkle of her eyes and her moistly parted lips. She looked up into his face, where the leaping flames produced sinister reflections, emphasizing his harsh bone structure, the high cheekbones and the strong thrust of jaw now flickering and dancing before her bedazzled eyes.

Sometime during the next song Russ stretched his arms lazily in the air and then dropped one casually around Cynthia's shoulders. By the end of the next song she had moved closer to him and was lightly resting her head on his shoulder. She hadn't brought a sweater with her, and his body heat felt so necessary to her well-being that she didn't care if some curious guest or gossipy staff member spotted them cuddled together in front of the campfire.

"Mr. Fielding, I left my little girl with a baby sitter. I'm going to have to mosey on home now," Hank said quietly as soon as he'd finished his last request.

"Go ahead, Hank. That was real nice of you to stay on and let Cynthia sample some of your best."

Cynthia lifted her head sleepily and murmured, "It was beautiful, Hank, just beautiful."

She could almost hear the last notes quivering in the still night air. Not wanting to break the mood by moving or speaking, she returned to her comfortable half-asleep position, watching with vague interest as Hank put away his guitar, slipped on his jacket, and disappeared into the circle of

172

blackness that surrounded them.

"The fire has almost gone out," Russ murmured. "You must be cold." He pulled her tighter against his side as he whispered into her hair, which wafted gently across her cheek in the breeze.

The words of all the songs that she'd just heard went tumbling across her mind. Love forever. Promises. Always yours. Your kisses. The lyrics drummed away at her heart, strummed across her mind. Don't leave me. I need your love. I want you. I love you.

Then she realized that Russ was speaking. "I think everything's going real well now that the construction contract is signed, don't you?"

"How can you talk about something like that at a time like this?" she said, lifting her head to stare at him, aghast. Obviously Russ wasn't haunted by the same romantic needs that had all her nerve endings afire lately.

"Do you mean you'd rather just sit here doing nothing? My favorite whirlwind is willing to suspend all her furious activity and just enjoy herself?" He seemed to find her attitude amusing, and a chuckle began rumbling deep in his chest until it erupted in peals of laughter, guffaws that shook her away from him slightly as he rocked back and forth in his mirth.

"Yes, if you don't mind. I could use a moment of rest," she said tartly. "It has been a long day, and those party plans have really swamped me."

"But the party is important, honey. It's to celebrate what you've begun around here. You should be proud to show it off to everyone."

She had never quite thought of it as her party, but it was a flattering suggestion. She sat quietly, considering what he'd said, as he pulled her close to him once more, apparently content to sit holding her until the moonrise.

"Russ Fielding! What are you doing?"

Helene's coming upon them so unexpectedly sent Cynthia's heart racing. The young woman's enraged, imperious tone was enough to make both of them spring to their feet.

"We've been waiting for you over in the cantina ever since the bonfire was over. And now I come to find you and what do I see? You're nuzzling your so-called employee," she sputtered angrily, searching for words and readily finding insults.

"Just a minute, Helene . . ." Russ began to protest, but she wouldn't listen.

"Mr. Wright has been looking for you, and he's a very important man. He's offered us a cruise next spring on his yacht, and he could send lots of his friends to stay here at the ranch." She turned to glare at Cynthia. "That sort of thing is supposed to be very important to you, isn't it? In fact, until this moment you had me convinced that making Haven Hills Tennis Ranch the best in Tucson was your most ambitious plan."

Helene's face was flushed, her eyes glazed. She was lurching about unsteadily on her high-heeled sandals, unable to get a good grip on the loose sand beneath her. She swayed forward, wagging her finger in Cynthia's face, and Cynthia could smell the sickly sweet aroma of rum on her breath.

"You have big plans, don't you, you ruthless little social climber," Helene continued, growing uglier by the minute.

"I'm going to take you home before you say something you regret." Russ almost shouted in an attempt to shock Helene into silence, taking a firm stride toward her that sent her cowering away from him.

"Oh no, Russ. I'm all right. Really, I'm

sorry." Suddenly she was trembling and contrite, her performance swiftly shifting to win his sympathy.

Russ grabbed her by the wrist, and she let out a helpless cry. "Oh, Russ, don't hurt me, please. I didn't mean any harm. It was just the shock of seeing you here alone with Cynthia. I just jumped to the wrong conclusions. Please forgive me, darling."

She put one hand to her head, brushed at a beguiling frizz of curls, and gave a flutter of mascara-thick eyelashes before falling limply against Russ's chest.

"She's passed out," Russ said. "I'll have to drive her home."

Cynthia wasn't sure if Helene had collapsed from too much drinking or was faking in order to shift this scene to her favor. But whatever the cause, Russell had swooped Helene up into his arms and had started walking away with her without another word, leaving Cynthia alone in the dark.

She sat back down by the fire, which was now an almost dead bed of gray ashes. Her eyes smarted from lingering smoke. She wanted to recapture the earlier warmth she'd felt here and she poked about in her memories, trying to rekindle the happiness that had been so abruptly shattered by Helene's surprising appearance.

Cynthia hummed a refrain she remembered, something about undying love. Then she picked up a twig and leaned over to poke at a smoldering stick in the fire pit. Why hadn't someone ever written a song called, "I Love You, Russ Fielding, and I Always Will," she wondered? She experimented with those words, whispering them to a plaintive tune.

She knew now she'd be singing this song to herself for the rest of her life. Her brief moments of happiness with Russ were over, and now there would only be sad songs for her. She didn't need any guitarist to strum the message for her.

Chapter Seven

Merry took one hand off the steering wheel to wave toward the cardboard boxes on the back seat. "What's all this stuff we have to take with us to the party?" she asked Cynthia, her passenger.

Cynthia was carefully following the map Helene had drawn for her that showed how to get to the Vickers's home near the Skyline Country Club in Tucson. As soon as they were allowed through the guarded gate, Cynthia knew they were in a most exclusive part of town. Every home was large, and the grounds were all expensively landscaped. The plants flourishing here would never survive untended in a desert climate.

"The easels are for the presentation to the press," Cynthia answered. "I had some beautiful watercolors done by the architect to show what the layout of the ranch will look like with the new additions. And I have press kits, name tags, new brochures, and lots of other materials."

"I hope Mr. Fielding appreciates what a wonderful job you've done," Merry said. "And I hope he notices your new dress."

"Kindly stop trying to play matchmaker," Cynthia said, giving her relentless friend a fond smile.

The Vickers's home was old and beautiful, set just below a sheer mountain rise to the north, with a wide brick entranceway at the end of a circular driveway surrounded by gardens. Dozens of uniformed people bustled about as Cynthia and Merry unloaded the car, putting the display materials in the long, high-ceilinged foyer that ran across the front of the immense house.

As Merry went to find Helene, to give her the typed timetable for the evening, which Cynthia had prepared, Mr. Vickers came through the foyer and noticed the carefully planned display Cynthia was setting up.

"I'm very impressed by this, little lady." He gave her a jovial pat on the back. "When Helene insisted we throw a big shindig, I'll admit I didn't see much point, but now I think we'll get lots of good press comments for the ranch, thanks to you."

"If that means full guest rooms all

winter, I'll be very happy." Cynthia smiled. "Then it will be worth all the money I spent and all the time we've put into it."

She looked around at the full bar that had been set up, the buffet table that was being loaded with platters and bowls, and the strolling musicians, who were tuning up their instruments. "It's going to be a wonderful party," she agreed with confidence, knowing how carefully she'd gone over every detail.

Mr. Vickers nodded enthusiastically. "Don't you think so, too?" he said to someone over her shoulder.

She whirled about, feeling a magnetic force pulling her in Russ's direction. He was standing just behind her, elegant in a black tuxedo. Though his attire was identical to what Mr. Vickers and most of the other male guests would be wearing tonight, she marveled at how the simple black suit looked so stunningly glamorous on him. His fair hair, freshly razor cut and shining, was brushed into layers of varying shades, from honey brown to spun-gold to almost pure white, emphasizing his blue eyes.

"You have a lot of bows to take this

evening," Russ said to Cynthia. "And you deserve them. You've worked hard to make this a success."

"Why, thank you," she said, hoping he wouldn't draw too much attention to her and embarrass her when the important guests arrived.

"Cynthia, there's a crisis in the kitchen," Helene called to her from just behind Russ. "You've forgotten something very important," she admonished in a shrill voice everyone was sure to hear. She began pulling Cynthia away from the two men, toward the kitchen door.

"You didn't bring Jean Claude with you!" Helene exclaimed dramatically, placing a handful of bright red fingernails in a tight grip on Cynthia's arm. "I told him he'd be riding over here with you tonight."

"You never told me that!" Cynthia protested. "The caterers I hired have everything under control. Do we really need him tonight?"

"Of course we need him! I want the press to see that we're introducing some culture and refinement to that barbecue operation Sonya runs out there."

"Then I'll call out to the ranch."

"That will just waste time. Here are my keys. Take my car. It's the dark-green Mercedes coupe."

"You want me to go pick him up?" she asked in disbelief, thoroughly aggravated.

"There isn't time to arrange anything else," Helene insisted stubbornly.

"Oh, all right," Cynthia agreed, angrily realizing she'd miss some of the best moments of the party. But she was determined that the evening would be perfect, down to the last detail.

By now Helene had led her through the kitchen to the door off the service porch, which led to the garages.

"Someone will have to stand at the door and give out name tags until I get back," Cynthia called. "And tell Russ that each press kit is labeled." Her mind was racing as she adjusted her plans to meet this unforeseen crisis.

"Believe me, Cynthia, I can take care of this party just fine until you return," Helene said, closing the screen door behind her.

Cynthia drove as quickly as she could in the unfamiliar car on the unfamiliar streets, getting lost only once, right near the country club. She turned on the radio to calm her nerves, but all she heard were frequent announcements of the time, and she realized that by now people must be beginning to arrive at the party.

The ranch was being run by a skeleton staff this evening since most of the others were involved in the party. Cynthia tried the kitchen first, but Sonya said she hadn't seen Jean Claude. Then she tried his room, but no one answered her knock.

She took a dime from her purse and went to the pay phone in the hallway. It took several minutes before the stranger who answered the phone could find Helene and bring her to the line.

"Yes, I know Jean Claude isn't there." Helene laughed as if an amusing farce was being played out for her entertainment. "Just minutes after you left he showed up here. He's such a resourceful fellow, he took a cab."

As sounds of the party filtered past Helene's voice, Cynthia clutched the receiver tightly. She was furious. "Well then," she said coldly, "I'll head on back."

"Oh, no! Don't do that. Jean Claude felt so bad that you'd gone all that way looking for him that he started right out to catch you. Merry's driving him. You must wait for them or things will really get confused." Helene giggled.

"But Helene, in just a few minutes, at eight forty-five, Merry is supposed to describe the new gift shop and show samples of the products." Cynthia checked her watch nervously.

"Oh, I've already done that for her," Helene interrupted.

"You've what!"

"I held up a couple of those cute little dolls and told them we'll be carrying designer ranch clothes as well as those touristy gift things. It went very well," she concluded happily. Disgusted, Cynthia thought of how her well-planned presentation had been mangled.

When Merry and Jean Claude finally pulled up in front of the ranch office, Cynthia was waiting in Helene's car.

"What's going on?" Merry called to her in a low, angry voice, as if she was ready to don war paint if what she suspected were true.

"Don't ask," Cynthia warned her with a furious outburst. "Just turn around and go back."

"I wish I knew less about kachina dolls and more about voodoo dolls," Merry quipped impishly before she drove away, and Cynthia laughed, realizing that Helene would have to be far more clever to fool that girl.

Cynthia drove slowly as she thought over Helene's plot to keep herself alone on center stage. She must have had a wonderful time at the party, making all the plans for expansion sound like her own, taking credit for all the hard work Cynthia had done. Worst of all, she'd robbed Merry of her chance to represent the new Indian crafts shop properly.

When Cynthia finally pulled up in front of the Vickers's house, there were very few cars left out in front. Near the front entrance she saw Russ and Helene bidding good-bye to the last guests, Helene modestly accepting the accolades for having put on such a lovely party.

Cynthia strode past them into the house without a word and began dismantling the display to load it into Merry's car. She made several trips to the car, but as she went out the door with the last load, she noticed that Russ and Helene were now all alone, partly concealed behind a small tree. Russ had pulled Helene close to him; her rounded body in her billowing red dress was pressed against him, and her hands were wrapped firmly around his neck. Cynthia knew she should walk on, but she paused to listen.

"Just hold me for a moment and don't say anything," Helene whispered provocatively.

"Helene, you know why I've stayed here in Tucson," Russ said. "You know what I want for the future." His voice was hoarse and compelling, as if he had pleaded his case like this many times before.

Helene's voice was only slightly slurred when she answered him. It was clear she'd had several glasses of champagne that evening. "I adore you, Russ. You know that. But that's not enough, it never has been." Her words mumbled to a stop, as if interrupted by a kiss.

Was Helene again refusing to marry him, Cynthia wondered, saying she didn't love him enough? But she had told Cynthia that she might soon consent to the delayed wedding, so why didn't she stop tormenting the man with her refusals? Cynthia couldn't bear to listen to any more and rushed on to the car, her eyes dimmed by unshed tears. What a miserable triangle she'd gotten herself involved in!

Merry was already behind the wheel of her car and the engine was running. Jean Claude, sitting beside her, still looked slightly confused by the crazy pace of the evening.

"I hope this is the last load," Merry said as Cynthia put a box in the back seat.

"Yes, I only have to go back and get my purse."

Merry leaned out the window. "You know what?" she said impishly, "I'm not waiting for you."

"No more jokes, Merry. I've had enough tonight."

The caterer's truck had just pulled away, and Merry tossed her head in the direction of the only car left parked on the street. It was the ranch station wagon that Russ had driven.

"No, I mean it. You can get a ride back with someone," Merry said with a gentle laugh, and she drove away, leaving Cynthia standing with a vexed expression on her face, planning suitable revenge upon her scheming friend.

She went back up the driveway toward the house, noticing with relief that Russ and Helene were no longer involved in their oblivious lovemaking in the front garden.

They must have gone inside. She opened the door quietly and went in search of her purse. Lights were still on everywhere, but there was no one in sight. Then Cynthia heard voices near the bottom of the stairs. Mr. Vickers was speaking to Russ and coming down the last few steps. "I made sure she got to bed."

"Do you think she's all right?" Russ asked with a sigh.

"Oh, yes. She just had herself all worked up. She'll be fine in the morning. But it breaks my heart to see her wrestling with this same old problem, denying the truth."

"Max, she has to grow up. She has to accept the situation. In the last few years she's been traveling so much that I didn't realize how far it had gone."

Cynthia wondered what Helene's problem could be. Whatever it was, both men sounded very concerned. She remembered the scene at the campfire and Helene's bright, overstimulated look this evening and wondered if she had developed a drinking problem. Disconsolately, Cynthia again considered the complicated emotional entanglements that kept Russ tied to his former fiancée.

"Cynthia, I thought you'd gone home by

now." Russ had turned down the hall and seen her standing in the shadows, lost in thought.

"I seem to have missed my ride. I was going to call a cab."

"I'll take you back with me," he said in a firm voice that brooked no argument. "I'm leaving right now."

"I have to thank Mr. Vickers for everything," she said.

"Tell him some other time. He's upset about Helene right now."

"Did she . . . I mean, I'm sorry if she got some bad champagne."

"Oh, she didn't have too much to drink, if that's what you're hinting at. What happened the other night at the bonfire was a rare occurrence, thank God."

Cynthia had to admire the gallant way Russ defended Helene, covering up her weaknesses. He walked Cynthia quickly to the car, then pulled to an abrupt stop beneath the gas lamp at the end of the driveway to step back from her and take a long look.

"Since I didn't see you much this evening, let me tell you right now I think that dress is absolutely smashing."

Cynthia ducked her head, suddenly shy,

unable to look directly into his eyes. "I wanted something special for tonight," she said, remembering with frustration the high hopes she'd had for the evening.

"It was a great party," he said as he held open the car door. After he got in and started the engine he continued, "It's too early to go home and just forget about it. I want to talk."

After driving a short ways, he turned off the main highway and headed down a bumpy road that seemed to go nowhere. "We'll take off our shoes and look at the moon and talk about the party and listen for the sound of a mean old coyote out there."

After a while the road became so rutted and jarring that he simply stopped the car. He switched off the headlights. "It will take your eyes a few minutes to adjust to the dark, but pretty soon you'll see all kinds of things out here in the desert. Most people think of it as nothing but a big barren space, but there's plenty of life here for anyone who stops to look for it."

Suddenly it looked as if their car was surrounded by a dozen giants with their arms thrown up in the air.

"Look at that saguaro cactus." Cynthia

laughed. "It sure seems menacing on a dark night. I feel like the posse has come to capture us."

Russ chuckled. "And that cactus has the prettiest little flower on it if only you could see it. And out there in front of us there are probably kangaroo rats running around in the dark, maybe even some deer. And there's probably an old gold or silver mine over there at the base of the hills. And underfoot there may be agates or garnets or tourmalines."

"Or peridots," she said, holding up her necklace to show him the pretty work Merry's uncle had done.

He turned sideways in his seat and reached over to take the necklace in his hands and examine it in the almost total darkness.

"Yes, there's beauty all around us tonight," he agreed.

His hands moved stone by stone around her neck, lingering against her skin as they moved, and her body quaked with thrilling response to his closeness. The lonely hours she'd spent dreaming of his touch were over. She was near him once more.

'This necklace complements your eyes," he said in a soothing drawl that made flattery sound so sincere. "I couldn't help noticing tonight how your eyes looked sage green. They're beautiful," he said, not making it clear to her whether he meant her eyes or the gems.

She closed her eyes for a moment, overcome by the heady perfumes of his masculinity, the musky virility that emanated from every pore of his body when she was close to him like this, arousing all her expectations and setting off complicated chain reactions that blocked off logical thought. Just when she thought his hands were about to move on and cool the warm skin on her neck and shoulders, he let go of the necklace and placed his hands behind his own neck to slide down in the seat as if it were a lounge chair. He stared outside again at the desert he loved.

Cynthia stirred uncomfortably, wishing she could turn off the fountain of passions he had put into circulation within her body once again. Just being alone with him in this desolate spot excited her, made her breath come in quick, anticipatory pants. Her need for him now was overpowering. All she knew was that she loved him and wanted him. She was incapable of thinking beyond that.

"Were you satisfied with how the evening went?" she asked finally, hoping to still her runaway emotions with conversation.

"You had things planned so beautifully that even without you it all went smoothly. Helene filled in where she could, but I wish you'd been there to see how everyone responded to all your work."

For a silent moment Cynthia watched a half-moon make irregular appearances from behind fast-moving clouds.

"Yes, it all went very well, indeed," Russ said thoughtfully. "I think this was probably the most important night of my life, Cynthia. On a personal level, I mean, not just because we snowed a bunch of travel writers."

Cynthia stiffened. Only one thing in the world could make Russ so happy. Perhaps she hadn't overheard enough to understand that conversation in the garden. Perhaps Helene had finally relented. Perhaps after Cynthia had walked on by she had told Russ . . .

"From now on everything's going to be better than ever," he said happily. "My life was pretty darn good, mind you, but now it's going to be awfully close to perfect."

It was becoming clearer to Cynthia that Russ had extracted some sort of promise from Helene this evening. Had she at last made the hard decision to throw away the footloose life of fun and gaiety and devote herself to the hard job of being Russ's helpmate in running the ranch?

Russ reached over and pulled Cynthia across the seat so she was sitting close beside him. "You're just the one I want to have here to share all this with me, honey," he said with a contented sigh. "Your coming out here to Tucson was a great idea."

She wasn't too sure of that. It seemed she'd set herself up for a permanently broken heart. Apparently Russ expected her to stay and toast her old friends at his and Helene's belated wedding. He didn't have any way of knowing what the sight of that happy bride and groom would do to her.

"We're going to turn that ranch into something special, indeed we are," he added softly.

Yes, he and Helene would make it a huge success. And he probably expected Cynthia to go right on tapping away at the adding machine while the Fieldings stood on top of their hill and drank champagne with VIP visitors, enjoying life. No, she would have to leave. It would hurt too much to stay and watch their happiness.

"You seem awfully serious this evening," Russ said. "Is it because you missed all the fun at the party?" He leaned down and lightly pressed his lips against her cheek. "I can make up for that. You're going to have your fun right now."

His hot breath singed across her face, finding its way under the hair at the back of her neck.

"Russ, don't," she protested weakly, her self-control slipping already.

"You are my sagebrush beauty, with your eyes shining gray and green, driving me crazy."

His hands slid down her body, caressing the soft jersey, sliding it sensuously across her skin beneath his heavy fingers. Her breasts swelled against the friction of the fabric, and she gasped with anticipation as the exploration of his slow touch intensified. She fell against him heavily and realized with a shiver of delight that he wanted her as much as she wanted him. But suddenly the shiver seemed a warning.

He wanted to have it all – to marry the

ranch owner's daughter and still play around with Cynthia. He probably expected to return from his honeymoon aboard some private yacht in some private cove somewhere and find Cynthia Price still perspiring at her desk, breathlessly awaiting her Friday night audiences with the boss. He wanted to marry the woman he loved, but still enjoy the partner he knew he could arouse so quickly.

"You can't do this, Russ," she blurted out into the darkness, reaching down to her breasts and taking each of his hands in hers to remove them forcibly from where they were distracting her.

"I will not let you ruin my life. I won't stick around your ranch waiting for you to sneak little moments of pleasure with me in parked cars. I won't settle for that."

"That's certainly not what I intend," he said, his voice languid but with a brooding undertone.

"I have to get on with my own life. Why, before long I'll be well enough to leave Tucson."

"Oh, you have bigger things in your future, is that it?" His voice held a warning.

"Yes, after what I've learned working

here at Haven Hills maybe I can go to work for some bigger guest ranch in Scottsdale or Phoenix."

"You can't relax and enjoy where you are, can you? You're always thinking ahead, reaching higher and higher for what you want."

"Is that what you think I'm doing?"

"How else would you explain your impatience to move on?"

He had shifted away from her with a sullen shrug, and now that he was back behind the wheel of the car, it seemed only natural to start it up and turn it around on the narrow, deserted road. Her side of the car seat felt cold now, in spite of what the misty film on the window revealed about the hot passions they'd both been feeling just a moment ago. She rubbed her hands up the side of her arms and around her neck, retracing the sensitive paths his hands had just traveled.

The sooner she left and got over these heavy, heartsick feelings she'd gained from learning to love Russ, the better off she'd be. She wanted to help Russ get the construction work underway, and then she'd move away and get another job.

Let Russ believe, if he wanted to, that

she could callously use what he'd taught her here to get a better job at a bigger guest ranch. Let him believe the old prejudices he refused to let go of about her driving ambition. It would be far better for him never to know her real reason for leaving, better that he never know that she'd fallen in love with him.

He would never know the devotion she could offer him. He would never feel the power of her consuming love. He would never experience the joy that their love could be. But, sadly, neither would she.

Chapter Eight

One side of the ranch quadrangle became a construction zone, but Cynthia arranged with the contractor to bring in hundreds of trees and plants in containers from a local nursery to shield the view from guests who had paid good money to come to Haven Hills for relaxation – not to watch cement mixers and ditch diggers doing their jobs.

"Cynthia, don't you think you'd better hire an extra gardener to keep that potted jungle of yours alive?" Russ asked her as she entered the office early one morning. "You can't water all of those yourself."

She had already spent over an hour walking around the freshly graded area where the new tennis courts would be laid out, pacing out every foot of the new guest wing to make sure the dimensions were just right before the workmen poured the foundations.

"Cynthia, your clothes are all dusty. Here, let me brush you off," Sonya insisted, jumping up from her desk. "I didn't see you at breakfast this morning, so I figured you were skipping meals again. I've left some rolls on your desk and a container of coffee."

"Thnks, Sonya. Are all these telephone messages for me?" Cynthia asked, taking a handful of papers with her as she followed Russ into his office to respond to his comment about the plants.

He sat down in his swivel chair and leaned back, a slightly bored smile on his face as he shot a rubber band across the room at a calendar on the far wall, looking for all the world like a sheriff in a quiet country town, resigned to too much desk work and not enough action.

"Honey, what are you going to do about the dust that's blowing across the tennis courts every afternoon? How much longer is that grading on the new courts going to be going on?"

"One question at a time, boss, please," she said with a sigh before taking sip of the coffee she'd brought in with her.

"As a matter of fact, any business matters I have to discuss with you can wait until our weekly meeting tomorrow night. There's only one answer I have to have now. What happened to your tennis game?"

"What do you mean?" she asked, reaching up with a tired hand to hook a limp strand of hair behind each ear.

"We managed to play a little tennis together before this construction project began. Now I haven't seen you in that skimpy tennis dress I like so much in several weeks."

Russ's chair creaked as he tipped it back and forth with his foot, watching her like a stern schoolmaster. His other foot, displaying a shiny expanse of cowboy boot, rested on his knee. A frown disturbed his usually sunny expression.

"You came out here to get healthy and strong, and now you're working too hard. I don't like it."

"Russ, you never saw me during a midwestern winter. You don't realize how my health has changed. I've gained weight since I've been here, and I haven't had any colds. And I thrive on hard work. It's more fun for me than all the tennis in the world."

She got up as if to leave.

"Sit down," Russ commanded, "and finish that coffee." He stood up and went out, bringing back a plate of sticky orange rolls, which he put on a corner of his desk just in front of where Cynthia was sitting. He removed the papers from her hand and, with a firm hold on her shoulders, leaned her back in her chair in a more relaxed position.

"Just take a minute out to have a bite to eat and make me happy, will you, sweetheart?"

"Oh, all right." She laughed. "But I have an appointment with the architect in a half-hour. Stop hovering over me, I'm just fine."

"You may say you're fine, but you don't look fine. I want to see you looking as pink cheeked and bright-eyed beautiful as you did that morning you woke up at my house."

"Russ!" She spoke quickly to warn him before he could say more. The door behind her was open, and she didn't want anyone to hear any references to the night she'd spent with him. But the sounds of telephone conversations and the typewriters in the outer room did not change their busy pattern in the least. "I wish you'd be careful what you say," she told him sharply.

"Is there some reason you don't like to be reminded of that night?" he asked her.

Of course, he was right. She spent every waking moment trying to push those lovely memories out of her consciousness and into some well-buried region of her heart.

"I don't want to get people talking about us, especially now that Helene is around here so much," she whispered, wondering if he could see the flush on her face.

"I'm not married to Helene, remember?" he said as if he were making a light joke out of her earlier misunderstanding about his marital status.

'But you obviously feel responsible for her," she said tentatively. She wanted to come right out and ask him if he still wanted to marry Helene.

"You know, there are weak people in the world and there are strong ones," he said. "And the weak ones seem to demand constant reassurance. When they start to droop, you just have to rush right over and catch them before they fall."

"And Helene is weak."

"She sure is. I didn't realize until recently just how dependent on me she's become."

"But what about the stronger people?"

"You just stand out of their way and watch them prosper," he said with an engaging grin.

"And you see me as one of those people?" she asked, not feeling at all self-sufficient at the moment.

"Yes," he said. "You'll always pull through, Cynthia."

And because of that, she could now see, she would never have much of Russ's sympathetic attention.

Cynthia was anxious to change the subject to a less intensely personal one. "Well, getting back to the tennis idea, I'll try to take some time out to relax over the weekend."

"See that you do. You look tired and frazzled."

At last Russ seemed satisfied that she'd taken time out to eat, and he let her leave the office and begin her busy day. She didn't have a chance to relax again until late afternoon, when Merry caught her darting across the lawn on her way back to the office from the tennis court site.

Merry pulled her to a stop. "I want you to come and sit down over here with me by the cactus garden for a minute," she said. "You can see the table in front of the cantina from here."

Cynthia didn't understand what Merry

meant, but she was too tired to argue. She followed dutifully. "Now, look at that. This is the fourth day this week that Miss Vickers has come out here all dolled up to spend the afternoon."

Cynthia looked over to where Russ and Helene were sharing tall, cool drinks at an umbrella table. Around them milled several ranch guests who occasionally drew near enough to throw Helene a compliment or entertain her with witticism. She was wearing a gauzy dress in a flowered print that set up a striking contrast to the riding outfits the women nearby were wearing.

"Cynthia, how long has it been since you've put on a dress?" Merry asked suddenly, surprising Cynthia. "In fact, how long has it been since you've combed your hair?"

Cynthia was deeply insulted. "Is there something wrong with my hair?"

'Nothing at all except that you've neglected it. You hardly even wear lipstick anymore."

"I've been busy."

"Yes, but here's a word to the wise. Don't get so busy that you ignore yourself. Because while you do all that work, someone else is taking the time to make the best appearance and get all the fun and the credit." She nodded in Helene's direction. "She's trying to charm Mr. Fielding, to make him think she's a great addition to this place."

"Merry, she doesn't have to charm Mr. Fielding," Cynthia protested. "She's had him branded as her own since she first met him."

"I'm not so sure, Cynthia. I've seen the way Mr. Fielding looks at you when you come rushing into the dining room or when you dash across the lawn on some errand. I think you might be able to show that Helene Vickers a thing or two if you'd slow down and give it a chance."

"Oh, you've had me in mind as a replacement for Helene since that first night I arrived here. But I've explained to you, Russ and I are all wrong for each other. He's much better off with her. Look at them. Look how perfectly suited to each other they are, laughing and drinking and talking together by the hour, while I'm rushing about, taking my every chore so seriously."

She said the words casually, but each one pained her, and as she joined Merry in leaning forward with her elbows on her

206

knees to stare dejectedly toward the cantina, her heart throbbed painfully and she wished she could be more like Russ, able to agree with him on every issue, able to share his temperament the way Helene did.

Clutching her list of things to do, she pushed herself to her feet and bid Merry a dispirited farewell, then hurried back to the office. Suddenly she turned on her heels and headed in the opposite direction, toward the bunkhouse. She was going to take a good look at herself in the mirror. Sonya had told her she looked dusty. Russ had told her she looked frazzled. And now Merry had told her her hair looked unkempt. It was time for a summing up.

She hurried to her room and slammed the door behind her, then turned as if dreading the enemy she must face and looked at the long mirror attached to the back of the door. It was true. She had let herself go. She had devoted herself so much to her work at the ranch that she looked a fright. No wonder everyone had been commenting on her appearance.

But was Merry right? Was there a point of dressing up and showing herself off to the best advantage in front of Russ? He was obviously physically attracted to her, she had to admit that. But could she use that small advantage and make him forget how unlike their personalities were? Was there a chance for her before Helene grabbed him off and made him legally and permanently her own? Maybe she should find out.

Already her eyes looked brighter. Tomorrow night she wouldn't trudge up the hill to their meeting in her rumpled jeans. She was going to have an evening with Russ that she could remember, even if things didn't work out and she had to leave here forever.

She was young, she was free, and she was supposed to have unlimited quantities of drive and ambition. So, why give up on life and love? Why not make a fight for it? If Helene wasn't ready yet to tell the world she owned Russell Fielding, then it wasn't too late. There was still time to win his heart away from her!

The next evening as Cynthia strolled up Russ's driveway she still felt the giant optimism that had filled her since yesterday. Her new dress of light sunset-pink voile billowed around her tanned knees in the evening breeze. After touring furniture showrooms in town with the architect that afternoon, she had taken time off to shop for the new dress and have her hair professionally styled. The new look was soft and layered, and she was pleased with the way it fell in a silky cascade down her slender neck.

When she got to Russell's house, she was surprised to find the front door standing slightly ajar. She pushed it open, calling his name, but there was no answer. Finally she searched the whole house, but found no sign of him.

The last place she looked was his bedroom, where she could smell the scent of his recently applied shaving lotion. His jeans and shirt formed a tumbled pile on the floor that suggested he had changed quickly out of them. She picked them up and carried them to the bathroom clothes hamper, finding the room still humid from a steamy shower. Russ must have been here just a short while ago, and then dressed and left.

If he was going to be late for their date, she decided she might as well enjoy herself while waiting for him. In the kitchen she found an open bottle of wine in the refrigerator, poured herself a glass, and went out onto the patio to watch the sunset from a comfortable lounge chair.

Almost an hour later she realized that the telephone was ringing. She remembered there was a phone in Russ's bedroom, so she stumbled through the dark house to reach it.

"Hello. Oops! Oh, I knocked over something."

"Cynthia, is that you? It's Russ. What's the matter?"

"Oh, I'm in your bedroom, and there's no light on in here, and now I've knocked over a stack of books."

"You mean you're in my bedroom in the dark and I'm not there? Something is definitely wrong!" he joked.

She grinned into the receiver.

"Where are you?"

"I tried to find you all afternoon to tell you that I have to cancel dinner. I decided to leave the front door open for you and call you there. I'm in town for some fancy shindig to benefit the Tucson Opera or Symphony or something. I was hoping to get through early, but it looks like I'm stuck here. I'm sorry you've been waiting for me."

"Oh, I don't mind."

"What have you been doing for almost an hour? Going over all those cost sheets of yours that we have to talk about?"

"If you must know. I've been sitting on the patio drinking wine and watching the sun go down."

"Doing nothing?"

"That's right."

"That's my girl! But now I want you to go down and get Jean Claude to heat you up something from the dining room for dinner."

"All right, guardian angel. Stop worrying about me and go back to having fun."

"This kind of fancy party isn't any fun. I'm just counting the minutes until I can get out of here. Oh, got to go. Bye, Cynthia."

He hung up so suddenly that Cynthia assumed someone had dragged him away from the phone. She felt a sudden emptiness as she put down the receiver, the sonorous melody of his voice gone. She rearranged his books on his night table, then began to wander through the dark house from room to room. She didn't turn on any lights. As long as it was dark, she could pretend that Russ was here somewhere, that he was waiting for her in the very next room, that he might speak to her at any moment.

Maybe Russ could get away sooner than he'd expected. She probably should wait for him awhile, just in case. In the living room, she turned on one small lamp near the front door, then went over to the plump sofas and sat down, content merely to sit and wait for him.

After a time the downy softness of the cushions behind her seemed more inviting, and she stretched back and closed her eyes. The room was almost dark, and the wine had made her sleepy so that within a few minutes she had drifted off into a peaceful fantasy land where a lush oasis stood in the center of a broad warm desert and cool water dripped into an inviting pond.

Later she sat up with a sudden start, realizing that Russ was going to be getting home very late. She would close her eyes for just a few more minutes and then she'd go. She slipped her feet out of her sandals and pulled her legs up onto the couch, stretching out to her full length before slipping into the deep sleep once again.

From somewhere in the furthest recesses of her mind she heard the sound of wheels grinding up the steep driveway outside and was dimly aware of an automobile engine turning over with one last roar before being silenced. A car door slammed. Then it was blissfully quiet again, and she let herself drift back into a comfortable sleep. She was sure it was a dream as she listened to footsteps and the sound of a door opening. Then she heard someone give a quick intake of breath upon discovering her on the couch. Was someone standing over her, watching as she uncurled one hand from where it rested beside her face, watching the seductive nature of her somnolent stirrings as she twisted the length of her body in sensuous appreciation of the cozy nest she'd found for herself?

The cushion she was lying on depressed slightly, and her eyes fluttered open only briefly to see Russ sit down beside her. To make more room for himself he placed his hands gently about her waist and lifted her like a sagging rag doll until she was lying on her back beside him.

Cynthia was far away somewhere, again at that desert oasis where movie extras wandered in billowing robes beneath swaying date palms. She was reclining in a tent, and an incredibly handsome blue-eyed captor was leaning over her, breathing unmistakable messages of desire into her face like a hot wind off the rolling sand dunes.

His exotic lover's hands were moving all over her gauzy dress, tangling it around her shoulders and knees as his insistent touch pulled her into the depths of passion. She sensed the powerful strength of him bent over her, his perfect control, and her heart beat wildly with the excitement of her dream. She was being taunted and tyrannized by his commanding touch, and she shivered with delight at the knowledge that she was in the hands of a master who would demand her total surrender.

She raised her arms above her head in an automatic gesture of submission, then drowsily lowered them, encountering the husky neck and shoulders of her dream hero close to her now as he descended to place his mouth on hers, forcing her head back into the pillows. She clasped him to her with instinctive fervency, twined her fingers through the springy hair that brushed down the back of his head in a wavy mass, and gave herself up to the throbbing, seeking intrusion of his kiss.

Pin pricks of pleasant pain dotted up her

spine, awakening her with a flow of erotic energy. Her hands moved insistently about his neck, pulling him close so that he lost his hold on the floor and fell on top of her on the couch, their kiss magnified by the movements of their bodies. His long, lean legs wrapped around hers, the fabric of his trousers rough against her bare thighs where her dress had been twisted away from her.

"Cynthia," he gasped. "Cynthia, I'm so glad you waited for me." He embraced her fully and lifted her toward him as he raised himself up slightly on the couch.

Cynthia shook her head to clear away the mists of exhausted sleep. Was she still asleep and dreaming that Russ Fielding was holding her in his arms, making love to her?

She opened her eyes languorously, blinking with confusion as she took in the strong face before her.

"I thought I was dreaming. I didn't know where I was." Her voice sounded thick and lower pitched than usual, and Russ laughed as he lowered her gently onto the cushions.

"You're right where you belong, right here with me. And now that I've got you where I want you, I'm going to have my way with you," he said with mock menace. He lunged forward and began kissing her neck, making a moist trail toward first one shoulder then the other. He was as unhurried as ever, his hands raking through her silky new hairstyle.

He took her shoulders in a firm grip and placed his mouth on hers again, and now she was sure she was kissing Russell Fielding. There could be no mistake. The kiss was cinnamon and harmonic chords on an upright piano and desert wildflowers blooming where flash floods had recently ravaged through a narrow valley. His pace was slow, his manner imperturbable, and he was unquestionably, as always, his own man, and a unique wonder to her. In some ways she was more fully awake—and alive—than she had ever been in her life.

Slowly his tantalizing mouth pulled back from hers, and his words came as softly and slowly as the drip of thick honey. "What are we hurrying this for? We have a long night ahead of us. I'm going to fix us a drink and then we're going to move this petting party to our favorite chaise on the patio until it turns too cold for us, like last time."

"Stay here. I don't want a drink," Cynthia protested in a mumble, tugging him back beside her as she gave a tired yawn.

"Honey, I love to see you relaxed, but you're darn near unconscious. I want to wake you up enough to really enjoy the music before we start this little dance we're going to do tonight."

He got up, laughing to himself, then stood watching her collapse into the cushions, her legs still curved seductively. He tugged his tie loose, unbuttoned the top fastening of his white dress shirt, and wriggled free of the confinement with a happy look.

"You know, when you give a sexy yawn like that, all I can think about is bedtime," he said softly. Her thoughts were running in the same direction, but she was determined not to rush things, to follow the pace he set.

Russ disappeared into the kitchen and, stretching wider awake, Cynthia decided to see if she could fix them a snack and make this a leisurely midnight picnic. She got up off the couch slowly, slipped into her shoes, and pulled her dress and hair back into some sort of order as she went to join him, a glowing smile on her face as she considered the night ahead.

But as she stepped up into the entry hall, she stopped suddenly, thinking she heard a muffled sound outside. It was too late for visitors, so she continued on, then stopped again, realizing that someone was placing a key in the lock. She stood in stupefied fascination as she watched the doorknob turn and the door slowly open.

For several seconds there was total silence as the two women stared at each other in utter shock. Helene Vickers, dressed elegantly in a black crepe cocktail dress with a front so deeply plunging that her bulging breasts peeked provocatively over the neckline, was standing in the doorway with a key still in her hand. Under one arm she carried a small satin evening bag, and in the other she held an overnight case. Obviously Helene had her own key to Russ's house and had come prepared to spend the night with him.

The full realization hit Cynthia like a tidal wave.

Helene was not just Russ's college sweetheart, holding him off for years, resisting his romantic pleas to marry him. She was his *mistress*! She was used to coming and going from his house at will. She was his live-in lover, available whenever he wanted her. And someday soon she would be his wife.

Cynthia knew she should have accepted these facts before now, but she'd kept her eyes closed to the blinding truth. Now she had to face it. Russ and Helen had worked out a relationship long ago that satisfied both of them, and there was no room in that tight circle for Cynthia Price and her dismal hopes for love.

Chapter Nine

"What are you doing here?" Helene demanded, obviously as surprised to see Cynthia as Cynthia was to see her. "Russ and I had planned a perfect evening alone together. Now you show up in the middle of the night and spoil everything." Her eyes were wide and she was breathing heavily and moving from side to side trying to get around Cynthia and into the house.

"I had a meeting scheduled with Russ tonight. I waited for him all evening. I guess I fell asleep."

"I suppose that's an attempt to explain your disheveled appearance," Helene said accusingly, slipping past Cynthia and closing the door behind her.

Now Cynthia began quickly putting the clues together. Russ had come home dressed in a conservative dark suit, having told her he was at a fancy society party in Tucson. He and Helene had probably been at the party together.

Oh, they had a perfect arrangement all

set up. Until Cynthia came along, that is, with all her foolish dreams of rearranging their foursome into a more pleasing pattern. She was the odd man out and had been since her arrival. The sooner she left the better.

Helene dropped her keys on a hall table as if by habit and placed her night case on the floor with a loud thump, as if to reaffirm her territorial rights.

"I thought Russ and I had saved the very best part of this evening until last," she said, adjusting the neckline of her dress to further reveal the dramatic cleavage.

"You've made it clear that I'd only be in your way, so I'll be leaving," Cynthia said. She didn't want to prolong the agony by one more minute. She couldn't bear to face the two lovers together, knowing the truth of her unexpected and untimely interference in their plans. She hurried out the door.

As she stumbled down the hill, blinded by sudden tears, she wished she were still asleep and that her confrontation with Helene had been only a nightmare from which she would soon awaken. But the pain of her shameful humiliation was very real.

Once again Russ had taken advantage of

the desire that sprang up so easily between them. He had played with her, enticing her awake with his kisses, all the while intending to continue his more important plans as soon as Helene arrived.

Russ had admitted he responded to Helene's weakness, feeling a need to be supportive of her. But now it was clear his feelings went far beyond mere chivalry. Helene's unhealthy dependency on Russ was like a sticky spider's web that she'd woven skillfully around him, making him a willing victim.

Cynthia spent the night tossing and turning in bed. Her cheeks were still damp when the sun came up and, looking out her window across the barren landscape, she felt as empty as the desert and impervious to the sun's warmth.

Shortly after dawn she dressed for the day and ate a hearty breakfast in the dining hall. She drank a second cup of coffee, ladled extra strawberry sauce over her flapjacks, and took five pieces of bacon. Yet as she walked briskly toward the office, she had already forgotten that she'd eaten.

Even though it was Saturday, she intended to spend the entire day at work. The sooner she organized her projects, the

sooner she could leave the ranch. She spent an exhausting morning bent over her account books and the adding machine.

It was almost noon when she looked up for the first time, surprised to see Max Vickers, a bulging briefcase in his hand, heading across the room towards Russ's office.

"Russ isn't here this morning, Mr. Vickers," she called.

"It's you I came to see," he said over his shoulder. "I kind of suspected I'd find you behind your desk even on the weekend. Come on in here and let's talk."

He took off the western-style hat he wore with his conservative gray business suit, then lowered his bulk carefully into the chair behind Russ's desk.

"Has something gone wrong with the financing for the addition?" Cynthia asked.

"No, no, that's all proceeding very smoothly," he said with a sigh. "I've come to tell you that I've decided to let Russell buy the ranch."

"Why, Mr. Vickers, that's wonderful!" she exclaimed. "He'll be so pleased – "

"Now, just a minute. You realize he'll be tying himself to one heck of a long mortgage, especially with these fancy

223

additions added into it."

"He can pay it off if he keeps the rooms filled with paying guests," she said enthusiastically.

Max Vickers looked up at her quickly, his jowls working nervously as he clamped his teeth open and shut. "Are you referring to the nonpaying guest who stayed here last night?" he asked after a moment.

Cynthia was confused. "Why, no. I don't know what you mean."

"I mean the young lady who spent the night in room 142. My daughter, Helene. I've just been over there to see her and we've had a little talk."

"Mr. Vickers, I didn't mean your daughter. I didn't know she stayed in one of the guest rooms last night."

"Well, she did, and I've told her that from now on she's not to spend so much time out here at Haven Hills. It will be Russell's place, and she's to leave him alone."

"But why?" Cynthia stammered, too confused to follow completely what he was saying. Had she been wrong? Maybe Helene hadn't spent the night up at Russ's house after all.

"I'll be very frank with you, Cynthia,"

224

Max Vickers continued. "For years I've waited to see my daughter marry Russell Fielding. For a while I thought there was a real chance for it. When Russell agreed to stay on in Tucson and run this place, I thought he'd relent someday. I thought he'd come to regret canceling the wedding.'

"You mean it was *Russ* who called off the wedding?" she asked, an excited tremor in her voice. Helene had told her she had called it off. Mr. Vickers didn't seem to notice her shock and went right on.

"I underestimated that man's commitment to a decision. The years went by, but Russell didn't change his mind. Helene seemed reconciled at first and kept busy traveling around the world, but lately she's become more and more attached to Russell, more determined to make him change his mind. This last month it's been pitiful to watch.

"The night of the press party at our house she got so upset over Russell that she ran upstairs in tears. I guess she declared her undying love for him once again, but that didn't sway him. I love that boy like a son. I can't get mad at him for what's happening. If he doesn't love her, then he'd make a terrible husband, that's for sure.

225

But she can't see that. He's the first man she's ever wanted that she couldn't get."

"Mr. Vickers..." Cynthia stood up to leave, afraid that he would later regret saying such personal things to her. But he looked up and waved her back into her chair, apparently relieved to have someone with whom to share his anxieties.

"Then there's what happened last night," he said. "She insisted at the last minute that Russ, instead of me, take her to the party. And then some time after he'd dropped her off at home, I found out she went traipsing after him, following him back here to the ranch uninvited. This has got to stop." He slammed his fist down on the desk, scattering Russ's unorganized stacks of paper all about. "That's why I'm selling Russell the ranch, cutting him loose from all his ties with me, freeing him from whatever feelings of responsibility he has toward my daughter. He's a decent and compassionate man. I think he feels sorry for Helene, but he's in a bad position. He can't talk to the boss's daughter quite as honestly as he'd like to and make her face the fact that he's no longer her fiancé and that he'll never marry her."

"You think all he feels for Helene is

some misguided sort of pity?" Cynthia asked, her eyes bright with attentiveness.

"I had closed by eyes to it until you came along."

"Me? What did I have to do with it?"

"Now I've seen how Russell's eyes light up when he speaks of your vitality, your ambitions for this place. And I've seen how your plans fire up his own imagination. I've seen what the right woman can do for him."

"Mr. Vickers, I think you're wrong," she disagreed. "Russ and Helene have a lot going for them. They're very compatible. Russ isn't comfortable with me. We're as different as night and day. All I do is bug him with my hectic activity and my planning ahead. He resists everything I try to do around here. We fight all the time."

"My wife and I were total opposites too, and we had lots of fights," Mr. Vickers said, his pale eyes staring off into space with a dreamy expression that reminded Cynthia of his daughter. "But it's making up after a disagreement that makes it all worthwhile." His fond remembrances brought a youthful tautness to his wrinkled face. "There's a certain tang to a relationship like that, knowing how you

227

temper each other's extremes, knowing how you complement one another. That can't be beat! No, Helene and Russ are too much alike. When they're together they sit down and do nothing, and Russ is miserable. You're good for him, Cynthia," he concluded.

Cynthia said nothing, but her heart was soaring.

"I'm telling you this, pure and simple, to try to save my daughter before it's too late. You can tell by looking at her where her life is leading – chasing after men all over the world, having these silly flings and then running back to Russell for solace. When you came on the scene, she began pushing herself on him shamelessly. She was frantic, thinking she'd loose her safety net. I know he feels bad about it, but you can't ask a man to marry someone just to solve her problems. Not when he loves someone else."

Loves someone else! The words echoed in Cynthia's mind as Mr. Vickers gathered up his belongings to leave. Loves someone else? Was Russ in love with her? Cynthia's thoughts were in such a whirl that she was hardly aware of saying good-bye to Mr. Vickers. After he was gone she sat down in

Russ's chair and leaned back to think over all that the older man had said.

She still couldn't totally accept Mr. Vickers's assessment of the situation. Perhaps he was right, and it had been Russ who had canceled the wedding, who was still resisting marriage to Helene. When Cynthia considered the situation from that perspective, many things made sense to her.

But she couldn't accept the startling proposition that Russ might be in love with her. It was too wonderful to consider, too farfetched to be true, even though it was the very miracle she was hoping for. She rolled and tumbled the new information about in her thoughts, trying to make sense of it.

A while later she realized that all the mental stimulation had made her ravenously hungry, as everything did lately. She would get something to eat first and then decide what to do next.

Knowing it was too late to be served lunch in the dining room, she went to the kitchen to fix herself a sandwich from the leftovers, filling a tray with cold roast beef, bread, and condiments. Jean Claude was busy making up a plate of thin crepes,

229

happily singing to himself. Cynthia followed him through the swinging doors into the deserted dining room and spotted Helene slumped over at a table near the doors.

"Here you are, mademoiselle," said Jean Claude to Helene. "I hope this cheers you up. A late brunch of crepes with apples Normandy." He proudly placed a steaming plate in front of her.

Helene raised her head slowly. "After the lecture from my father this morning," she said, "I appreciate the tender loving care." She sounded sad, less stridently assured than usual. "Thank you, Jean Claude," she added with an appreciative smile that sent her favorite cook hurrying back to the kitchen mumbling something about making more crepes for her.

As Helene caught sight of Cynthia, she quickly masked her distraught expression. Suddenly she was full of childish bravado. "Come and join me, Cindy," she called gaily. "I think you owe me some sort of explantion about last night. I want to know what you were doing waiting for Russell at his house until all hours of the night."

Helene's continued bluffing, in spite of her father's talk with her, made Cynthia furious. She plopped heavily down on a chair full of angry energy. "If you remember, Russ and I have a regular Friday-night meeting scheduled," she said through clenched teeth.

"You were waiting for him so you could throw yourself at him, you home wrecker!" Helene sputtered, but there seemed to be less fire than usual behind her outburst.

"You can't accuse me of being a home wrecker, Helene," Cynthia retorted. "You and Russ have no home to wreck, remember? You aren't married to him."

Cynthia's conversation with Mr. Vickers had made her more bold. Whereas before she'd believed that Helene had the stronger claim on Russ, now she dared to believe that Russ might love *her*.

"Russ and I will be married!" Helene insisted. "I'm just waiting for the right time."

"You're waiting for him to ask you, isn't that more like the truth?"

"We can work things out. We had a long talk about that last night. Oh, it was a wonderful evening," Helene said with a wistful smile.

"I understand you spent last night in room 142. I had no idea that room was so special," Cynthia replied calmly, taking a big bite out of the sandwich she'd put together. She knew her unrelenting attitude toward Helene's fantasies was harsh, but she felt she had to shock her into admitting the reality of the situation. Helene had lived for too long in a dream world of her own making.

In the bright light coming in the dining room windows Cynthia could study her former friend more critically than she had before. Helene's extra weight looked less flattering than Cynthia had thought at first. No wonder Helene's father wanted to turn her life around as soon as possible. Helene adjusted her curls as she said, "It's only a small misunderstanding that has kept us from getting married. So if you think Russ could ever fall in love with you, you're crazy. He knows what happened to your first husband, and he could never love a woman like you. He knows you drove Chuck away with your ruthless ambition, with the way you tried to run his life. Years ago, long before you two even went to live in Illinois, Chuck was miserable."

"That's not true." In spite of her distrust of Helene, Cynthia began to feel threatened by the other woman's accusations.

232

"I've told Russell all about poor Chuck," Helene went on. "Your husband told me how you pushed and pressured him to get out there and make a million dollars for you, and look at the way you've tried to run things since you came here. You heard Russ was going to inherit millions of dollars from that Texas grandfather of his, and you came here to get a part of it for yourself. Now you're adding on more tennis courts than we'll ever need and putting that little friend of yours into a gift shop business. I don't know why Russell doesn't just throw you off the place."

Helene was flushed from exertion. As her final words hung dismally in the air, she fell back against the chair with the look of a cornered soldier who has fired of all his ammunition, but knows it hasn't been enough to dent his adversary.

Cynthia finished the battle with quiet, carefully chosen words. "Russ has put up with all my plans and ideas because they're his dreams, too. And he's put up with me because he loves me."

She was amazed at how easy it was to say the words. It seemed the most natural thing in the world to acknowledge finally that Russ loved her – although when Mr.

Vickers had suggested it, she hadn't believed it.

Helene covered her face with her hands, her gesture one of defeat. "I know Russell doesn't love me," she admitted. "But I depend on him. How can I live without him? He's always been here. When things didn't work out, I could always come back to him."

"Maybe that's why things didn't work out for you," Cynthia suggested quietly. "It's been too easy to come running back to your college boyfriend. Maybe you need to let go of the past and get on with your own life." She reached out to pull Helene's hands gently away from her face.

"That's what my father told me this morning," Helene said, giving Cynthia a searching look. "He told me I have to face the truth and tackle life on my own."

"It won't be as hard as you think."

"Do you really love Russ?"

Cynthia nodded.

"Have you told him?" Helene asked.

"Not yet."

Helene seemed to be considering something. She took a deep breath and exhaled slowly. "Why don't you go find him right now and tell him?" she said at last. "He's out riding. He went up to that old mine on the outcropping of rocks just beyond his house."

"You want me to?" Cynthia asked, greatly surprised.

"There's no way I can hang onto a relationship with Russ." Helene's expression softened, the anger and bitterness having drained away from her face. "Long ago I destroyed any love he felt for me. But he's been kind to me, kinder than I deserved, I guess because he's so fond of my father. I want him to be happy, and you can make him happier than he's ever been." She pushed away the plate in front of her and sat up straight in her chair. "Well, that wasn't as hard to admit as I thought it would be," she said with a heavy sigh.

Cynthia rose to her feet and went to stand behind Helene. She gave her friend's shoulders a quick squeeze. "We're adults now, Helene. Maybe we can all find the happiness that escaped us when we were younger. We all know ourselves better now. We can make the right decisions."

Helene was looking into the distance, her pale eyes dreamy. "Russ takes his horse right into the mine with him and loads up his saddlebags with rocks," she said. "He thinks he'll find a gold nugget. Isn't that just like him?" Her voice caught. "He's always an optimist, always believes the very best is going to happen to him. Well, maybe this time it has. Now, go on, Cindy. Go find him."

Cynthia didn't need to be told twice. She hurried to the stables where the head wrangler gave her a mare that was as anxious to be on its way as she was.

A rocky path led up the side of the slope toward the mine, and Cynthia stayed on her horse until it became too steep. Then she slid off and began hiking, leading the horse by its halter until she saw some old boards that appeared to have once been a mine entrance.

Russ had explained to her that the Arizona hillsides were peppered with old glory holes that had been blasted out by hopeful prospectors. Around campfires, local people loved to tell and retell stories of missing lodes that were always exceedingly rich – like the Lost Dutchman, the Frenchman's, or the Mine with the Iron Door. One of Russ's favorite hobbies was to visit nearby ghost towns that had risen to brief prosperity back during the boom-and-bust days of gold fever in Arizona. He had told her about Jerome, Vulture Mine, Bumble Bee, and Dos Cabezas. But she hadn't known there was an old mine right here on the ranch property for him to explore. When she arrived at the entrance, a trail of hoof prints in the dust indicated that Russ had already gone inside.

The timbers supporting the entrance had slipped with age into jagged angles, but the opening was still large enough so that she could easily enter the dim cavern, even leading her horse behind her. Once inside, her eyes quickly adjusted to the lack of light. Rotting old timbers supported the large main room and several hallways jutting out at odd angles. Remnants of metal rail-road tracks protruded here and there under her feet, and she knew that this was where the loaded mine cars had left the mine with their precious cargo of ore or their worthless piles of blasted rock.

Venturing farther, she headed down the largest passageway, investigating its steeply inclined recesses.

"Russ?" she called. Her voice echoed back at her with a hollow sound, coming from so far away in the darkness that she grew frightened. The mine must run into the hillside for hundreds of feet!

"Russ, are you in here?" she called again. "I'm coming to find nuggets of gold with you."

Her voice seemed to reassure the horse, and it gave her some added courage herself as she took several more steps into the narrow tunnel. The closed space was beginning to make her feel a bit claustrophobic, and she knew that no one could possibly be ahead of her where the mine became darker and darker.

"Well, time for us to turn around and head on out of here, don't you think?" she asked her animal, stopping to reach up and pat her neck before trying to turn her around in the tight space. She gave a nervous whinny.

Just then she heard a small scurrying sound, as if hundreds of tiny pebbles had suddenly been loosened by the horse's neigh. Immediately the horse threw back her head in alarm and began stamping her feet in an effort to escape the enclosed space.

"Steady, girl. I'll get you out of this. Come on now," Cynthia murmured, trying to sound more calm than she felt.

But her words had no effect on the big animal, who jerked free of her hold on the bridle with a backward lunge and began desperately trying to escape. As the mare pawed the ground to get her bearings, she loosened great pits of soft gravel, which sprayed into the air.

Finally she succeeded in turning around, and she disappeared down the tunnel. The sounds of slipping sand increased where her hooves had begun to form a trench. All at once Cynthia realized that a support beam on the side wall had been loosened, and was creaking torturously, splitting in two as the decayed wood collapsed beneath the weight of the beams above it.

In seconds a cascade of splintered wood, rocks, and sand was all around her. Cynthia was thrown against the far side of the tunnel, the sound of the falling debris becoming deafening as it echoed throughout the cavern. To Cynthia it seemed it would never stop, that the tumult would go on forever, throwing debris at her, burying her beneath the rough materials that ripped her clothes, until the whole mine had caved in on top of her.

But miraculously the ricocheting rocks slowed to a stop – just as an almost suffocating pile of sand slid around Cynthia's body. Thick dust filled the air, and she choked and gasped for breath as it slowly settled and she was finally able to assess her situation.

Suddenly panic filled her. She couldn't move! Her legs were caught beneath a heavy load of broken timbers and fallen rocks. Although she could see the small opening that remained clear of debris just ahead of her, she couldn't possibly reach it. She was trapped! And if more rocks began to slide, even that small exit might be closed off to her. Her desperate situation would be resolved for good then.

From far away she heard the noisy clatter of her horse, still struggling to find a way out of the mine. Then it became deathly silent, and she knew that she was alone.

"Oh, Russ, where are you?" she whispered into the darkness. "Oh, Russ, I need you." She pressed a perspiring cheek against the rough stones beside her face and closed her eyes as the futility of her situation settled over her like a heavy weight.

Chapter Ten

It was a long time before Cynthia made even a small attempt to move from under the rocky grave that had trapped her. For the first few minutes she was afraid to breathe deeply, for the entire vault of beamed ceiling above her seemed in imminent danger of giving way. Every now and then streams of fine dirt sifted down on her through unseen cracks over her head, substantiating her fears about the unstable nature of the old tunnel.

But she couldn't just wait to die. She had to try to free herself or she would go crazy lying there, letting fear get a more insistent grip on her.

She was incensed by the injustice of her plight. Just when she had been about to reach out and grasp the happiness that life seemed to offer her, a capricious fate had sent her into this dangerous place from which she might never emerge.

Gradually she began to wriggle her toes and flex the muscles of her legs to find out in what position they were bent. Cautiously she moved her arms until they came easily free of a few loose rocks that had fallen on top of them.

A heavy piece of splintered wood slanted across Cynthia's body, apparently the main board that was trapping her legs. Now that she could get a good hold on it she began to tug it out from under the pile of sand. But a burst of sand started slipping immediately down the wall behind Cynthia, where the other end of the beam was resting. Her efforts seemed perilously liable to begin another avalanche.

Overcome with disappointment, Cynthia tipped her head back and gazed through the narrow crawl space left between the passageway in which she lay and the outer room. Looking past it, she could see the mine entrance, which appeared like a lighted archway with brilliant afternoon sun slanting across the floor.

Cynthia tried to calm her fears by breathing in and out slowly, willing herself not to give up hope. And then suddenly a wide shadow moved in front of the shaft of light, blotting it out. The silhouette seemed almost man-like, frozen in position there, and Cynthia wondered briefly if her terror

242

was making her hallucinate.

Straining to hold her head in the same position, she blinked the dust from her long eyelashes and watched intently. The air was filled with fine particles of settling debris that shone like gold in the sunlight and surrounded the hovering shadow with a radiant cloud, tempting her with freedom, promising she would no longer be alone. She weighed the risks of crying out within the rotting walls.

"Is someone there? Can you hear me?" a voice bellowed through the long, echoing chambers, sounding far away.

"Help!" Cynthia called weakly. Her throat was so dry that she could hardly say the word. "Help me. I'm trapped."

"Cynthia, is that you?" The huge form moved out of the light and began making its way toward her through the mine.

At first she couldn't believe it. Then she let joy wash over her as she realized Russ had come to save her.

"Russ, be careful!" she called hoarsely. "There's been a cave-in. Something might fall on you."

"I'm coming, Cynthia. Don't try to move. I'll get you out of this." His voice was like a soothing balm.

His hurried footsteps crunched over the sandy floor of the outer room and then down the passageway, coming closer and closer. The confined space transformed his every sound into trumpeted calls of reassurance.

Russell was barely able to fit his wide shoulders through the small opening that now led to her tunnel, but he carefully hunched through, crawling on bent elbows, and emerged just a few feet away from her, a dirty but welcome sight.

"Russ, I'm so glad you've come! I figured you'd left the mine, that I'd missed you. I didn't think anyone would ever find me. I was so frightened."

"Don't try to move," he warned her. "And don't say another word! Shock waves of any kind could bring this whole mine down on top of us."

Russell began picking debris up off of her as if he were playing a game of pick-up-sticks, paying the utmost attention to every move he made. Whenever he released a chain reaction of movement, he stopped what he was doing to try another approach. Soon he was removing the large beams that had trapped her in their viselike grip, and he used them to shore up the beams still in place over their heads.

"Do you think you have any broken bones?" he whispered as he began digging the loose sand out from around her legs, using his two hands like a giant scoop.

"No, my legs seem fine. I'm so glad you . . ."

"Shh," he cautioned. "No more talk."

There was so much she wanted to say to him. The strain of holding her words inside was almost unbearable. She wanted to scream her thanks to him for saving her, to sob on his shoulder and release all her bottled-up fear. She wanted to blurt out her love for him, to let him know what dark mines she would walk through for him if he was ever in danger. But even a slight wince or sigh from her brought a stern look of warning that convinced her their safety depended on her keeping still.

Soon they would be outside. Soon she could say everything. Her legs were almost free now. She could feel his hands scraping through the dirt along her right thigh. Except for a moment of tingling numbness down her limbs, she seemed in perfect condition.

"Okay, you're all uncovered," he said quiely. "Now move slowly. Make sure you're not hurt more than you think." Russ was bent over her, his face taut with concern.

"I'm fine," she whispered back. "See, I can move. Nothing even hurts." There was a long rip down one leg on her jeans and her flower-sprigged gingham blouse was in tatters, but her body seemed unscathed except for a few slight bumps and bruises.

"Follow me. The sooner we get out of here, the happier I'll be," he said.

She crawled behind him as he slowly and carefully made a path for her. Then, after what seemed like endless minutes, he was pulling her by the hand through the high-ceilinged outer chamber and toward the cave entrance.

At first the sunshine outside blinded her, but as her eyes adjusted, she exulted in the sights around her – the cloudless blue sky overhead, the cholla cactus growing nearby with a cactus wren flying about it looking for a nesting place, the yellow brittlebush growing amid the rocks along the pathway. How precious it all seemed to her! She spun around, eager to throw herself into Russ's arms.

But she froze. He was leaning against the side of the hill near the mine entrance glaring at her.

"Why in the world did you go inside that mine by yourself?" he demanded. "You could have gotten yourself killed!"

"But I'm all right, Russ," she tried to reassure him.

Secretly she reveled in his concern. Did his anger mean that he really *did* love her?

She watched him warily as he dusted off his dark-brown corduroy jeans, a disgusted look on his face. He took off the blue scarf tied around his neck, inside the collar of his cavalry-style shirt, and wiped his dirty face and hands.

"It's just lucky I noticed the roan mare you'd been riding. She came trotting down this hill, heading for home like she'd just been scared by a jack rabbit. She was all saddled up so I knew someone had been out riding her, and I began to wonder if a ranch guest who didn't know any better had wandered off the trail and gotten into trouble."

He snapped the scarf back in place around his neck, the color making his blue eyes leap out at her, like an inviting cool pool after a hot desert trek.

"Come on, my horse is over here," he said. "You can ride back with me." He started off down the path to a little plateau just below them where his horse was tethered to an ocotillo tree.

Russ watched Cynthia limp down the hill toward him. "You are the filthiest, grimiest critter I've ever seen," he told her, reaching out to take her around the waist and lift her up onto his horse as easily as if he'd thrown a sack of oats into the corral. "I don't even know if I want you on my beautiful clean horse." But this time the trace of a smile curved his narrow lips.

Right at his eye level her bare leg showed through the slit in her torn jeans. He reached over and gave it a hearty slap, as if to let her know his anger with her was merely protective, and then he swung up onto his horse and gave a few clicking sounds.

Cynthia leaned back against Russ's broad, warm chest. As she did so, he took one hand from the reins and curled it about her waist, holding her securely close to him so that he could dig his heels into the horse's flanks and bring them to a brisk trot without dislodging his passenger.

"Do we have to go so fast?" Cynthia complained. She wanted to enjoy the serene beauty of the late-afternoon desert scenery around them – and besides, her bruised body ached with every jolt of the horse.

"It will be sundown pretty soon, and I have to get back to the ranch. You know as well as I do that the contractor leaves at six o'clock.'

'But you don't have to be there to wave good-bye," she pointed out.

"I like to look over the day's work with him," Russ insisted. "You may not have noticed, but since we started the addition I've taken a very active part in supervising. Since you arrived here I've come to realize how proud I am of Haven Hills and how much of my life is wrapped up in its success."

"I'm glad to hear that," Cynthia reassured him, "but I was hoping we could take the long way home and enjoy this ride." She almost gasped aloud as they bounced over a particularly rough area.

"You want to take the long way home? Do you realize you're asking me to neglect my ranch duties?" Russ asked with mock horror. "I can't believe I'm really hearing Cynthia Price, that hard-driving career woman, trying to lure me away from my new sense of devotion to my work. Well, just to show you that I'm still my own boss,

I'll do it! We'll take this trail right here through the old grazing land and past the watering pond."

Russ slowed the horse to a more relaxed pace, and Cynthia rested against Russ, smiling as she contemplated the countryside she had learned to love so much. She sighed with contentment.

"Did someone really raise cattle on this land," she asked.

"Yes, Max Vickers's father ran a working ranch here."

"Then it's even more amazing that he's willing to sell you part of the land. That's one of the things I came to tell you. He came by today to say he's changed his mind. He's seeing a lawyer tomorrow to prepare some papers for you to look at."

"Well, well! I'll bet you jumped up and down for joy," Russ said, gripping her more tightly around the waist.

"I didn't say anything about whether you would accept the deal. That's up to you, Russ. You have to be sure you want to take on that indebtedness. Only you know how hard you want to work to build up this ranch."

"You don't even have any strongly worded advice for me on the matter?" he asked in a teasing tone.

"No, of course not. You have to do what makes you happy. I'm just pleased that the choice is available to you."

"So you're throwing the decision into my lap?" He was serious now. "That's not the act of a driving, controlling woman. I'm afraid I've misjudged you, Cynthia. You're hard working and not afraid to dream big things for the future. But if that's being pushy, I'll eat my hat."

"Why, thank you, Mr. Fielding," she said primly, squirming all the way around to look up into his face. In the bright sun she could make out a fine sprinkling of freckles across Russ's straight nose, which made him seem younger than his years, boyish and not at all formidable.

He must have been studying her face as well, for he leaned down and planted a kiss on the very tip of her nose.

"Ugh!" He pulled away. "A mouthful of dust and grit! I think I'm going to have to douse you in that pond when we get there. You are one filthy prospector."

Cynthia laughed. "I'd love a swim. How soon will we get there?"

"Just a few more minutes," he said, dropping the reins over the horn of the saddle to let the horse find his own way on the well-worn trail. Russ put both arms around Cynthia and held her small waist tightly.

"I had good reason to think the worst of you, Cynthia," he said. "Helene has been convincing me for years that you're a monster in disguise."

"Me? Why would she say such things?"

There was a moment of silence, then Russ said, "I guess I'd better tell you why I broke off all our wedding plans. I found my precious little bride to be had been having an affair with someone while she was engaged to me."

"Oh, how terrible!"

"It's worse than you think. While we were playing our innocent little doubles tennis games, and you and I were having all those rousing good arguments, it seems that Chuck and Helene were giving each other lustful glances behind our backs. You and I were being made fools of."

"Chuck? That's who Helene had the affair with? I can't believe it! We were happily married at that time. Why would he do it? Why would *she*?"

"He gave her the classic line – 'My wife doesn't understand me.' He convinced her that his life had been made miserable by an overly ambitious wife. Helene fell for it."

Cynthia was shocked. But as soon as she began to consider the idea, she realized it made sense. "Chuck would do anything to get what he wanted," she admitted. "And lying was his speciality."

The sharp pain caused by Chuck's betrayal began to subside. "You know, Russ, I'm glad I never new about this until now. Once it would have destroyed me. But I must be over Chuck emotionally as well as physically. His deceit no longer surprises me. It doesn't even enrage me. I can't take it personally because I know he didn't mean it that way; it's just the way he was. In this case, Helene suffered far more than I did. How did you find out about it?"

"After graduation, when we arrived in Tucson to be married. I overheard her calling someone in Chicago. She was telling Chuck all about the wedding plans and giggling about how she'd never forget the good times they'd shared during that exciting senior year. When I confronted her, she confessed everything, telling me in tears that she'd only been involved with Chuck very briefly and that she'd done so out of sympathy for him. She figured I'd forgive and forget, that the wedding could go on right as scheduled."

"But you insisted upon calling it off?"

"Yes. But she's never given up trying to convince me that what happened was all your fault, that if you hadn't been such a poor wife to that very noble and sincere man, he never would have turned to her for solace."

Cynthia gave a wry smile. Quite without knowing it she had been used as a scapegoat for all of Russ and Helene's problems.

Russ went on, his voice matching the rhythm of the horse's feet. "Then after I hadn't seen you for five years, you showed up here, and immediately the sparks began to fly. You got me all fired up about buying the ranch and making additions. You disagreed with every opinion that came out of my mouth. And I loved every minute of it."

"What a shock when I found out you'd never married Helene!" she said, her eyes sparkling as she remembered.

"And what a surprise when I found out you weren't married to Chuck! Suddenly it was a whole new tennis match. You certainly didn't seem to be the monster Helene had described. In fact, you were just what I was looking for in my life."

His voice was breathy, sending shivers of delight down her spine as it gusted hotly around her ears. "You know something?" he asked. "I like the *real* you a whole lot better than that awful picture of you that I've been carrying around trying to believe. Come to think of it, I *love* the real you."

Russ let his hands slide upwards so that they were delightfully spread just below Cynthia's breasts, his thumbs riding gently up across the tears in the cotton fabric. The tantalizing motion of his fingers, coupled with the rhythmic sway of her hips against his as the horse plodded on beneath them, reawakened all the sultry passion for him that she kept under shaky control at the best of times.

As they crested a small rise, a beautiful little valley rose before them, in the center of which stood a miniature lake hardly bigger than the ranch swimming pool. Filled with clear water, it reflected the violet blue of the afternoon sky.

"This old reservoir is now my private swimming hole," Russ said, taking up the reins again to lead his horse to a group of rocks around one end of the pond.

He slid off the horse and tied one end of

the bridle to a tree stump, then held his arms up toward Cynthia. She placed both hands on Russ's shoulders, glorying in the flex of his muscles beneath the rough homespun shirt. Then she swung her leg over the horse's back and let herself fall against Russ while he lowered her slowly to the ground.

All her nerve endings came instantly and clamorously alive as they responded to the inch-by-inch contact of Russ's rugged body. The large buttons that formed the square opening on the front of his cavalry shirt caught in the various holes in her blouse, slowing her progress even further and forcing her to squirm right and left in order to untangle herself. By the time her feet touched the ground, her blouse had been twisted and torn into a hopeless remnant, barely affording her any modesty beneath his searching gaze.

"You might as well take those clothes off, there's so little left of them," he said with a husky tone. "Do it quickly before I throw you in that water, rags and all." His voice carried an urgent, breathless message.

She turned her back on him, pulled off all of her clothes and left them in a pile at her feet. As he reached out to grab her, she let his fingers brush her bare shoulder for just a moment before she slipped away from him toward the pond. With a shallow dive she splashed into the cool water.

She swam away from him to the far side of the pond, enjoying the crisp bite of the cold water against her skin. She'd never gone swimming in the nude before, and she found it more stimulating, more exhilarating than she would have expected.

She tipped her head up toward the sky and, with her eyes closed, felt the balm of the sun's waning rays on her face. How glorious it felt to be alive on such a day! What a shame Russ wasn't sharing all the sensuous pleasures of his favorite swimming hole with her.

At the thought of him she turned to see if he was watching her swim. But though she scanned the entire perimeter of the pond, she couldn't see him anywhere. Then she noticed a second stack of clothes next to hers with Russell's cowboy boots thrown on top.

Just then water swirled beneath her and a large hand grabbed her ankle from below. Russ's fingers slipped quickly on her leg, then he let go, and with an explosion of water, he surfaced only a few inches away from her.

"Did you think I was going to let you have all the fun?" he demanded, breathing hard.

His smooth chest heaved in and out as Cynthia gazed at him, mesmerized. Now that she wasn't moving around, the coolness of the water began to affect her and she shivered slightly.

"Come here and let me warm you up," Russell said, treading water beside her. "I want you close when I tell you how much I love you, Cynthia."

She swam into his arms, and he kissed her so hard that she wondered if the water would boil up around them. She let herself sink beneath the water as soon as his lips left hers, slipping several feet down, feeling like a highly polished stone as she writhed teasingly from Russ's reach.

Even under the water she heard his whoop of laughter, and then he reached out to try to grasp her elusive body. His hands searched for every part of her, but she easily wriggled free. At last he grabbed a handful of her swirling hair and dragged her to the surface.

"Come here, little darlin'." He grinned

broadly at her. "There's nothing standing between us any longer. No misunderstandings, no jealous interference from others. Not even our clothes!"

He let go of her hair and she stayed willingly close to him, within the circle of his arms, which were supporting her in the water so that she didn't need to move in order to stay afloat. She stared into his eyes, which were afire with the reflection of the glowing sun behind her.

It felt so right to be with Russ like this. So good. All at once she realized that from the very first their opposing natures had made them ideally suited to each other. But they'd both ignored those instincts, bound by their commitments to Chuck and Helene. She sighed ruefully, realizing that that unfortunate pair had not felt restrained by any such pledges of loyalty.

Now Cynthia and Russ were at last free to take advantage of all that they had to offer one another. She would keep Russ motivated and help him build a meaningful future. And Russ would teach her to slow down and enjoy life's more subtle pleasures – like this swim, this sunset, those eyes of his trained on her with such intensity. It would take a lifetime of Arizona afternoons to appreciate all these pleasures.

"Marry me, Cynthia, and set things straight at last," he whispered in her ear. "Put the world in its proper order."

"Oh, Russ. That's all I want. I love you so much."

"When you marry me, all of this will be yours," he said with a laugh that resounded across the top of the water. "With me you get mortgages, half-built buildings, and a future full of hard work."

"But with you I get a chance to begin again, only this time it's going to be right. In fact, it's going to be perfect."

"Are you sure?"

"Well, there's just one small, tiny improvement that I can think of," she said, reaching out with one finger to trace a watery line down his cheek. "I think you look wonderful with a moustache. Would you grow it again for me?"

He pulled her into a tight embrace, and his laughter against her ear was like a burst of organ music, a wedding march played just for them in this beautiful desert setting. Their bodies thrashed together in the water, throwing sparkling drops of water into the air. Russ's wet skin glided invitingly over hers, slick and smooth. But at last Cynthia stopped the entertaining struggle to curve her naked body close against his, exulting in the familiar shapes and well-loved angles where she fit so comfortably against him.

At that moment the flaming sun poised for a brief moment on the edge of the horizon before making its final descent. It spread a golden shimmer of fire on the surface of the pond, lighting up Russ's face with amber flames and tinting the sky above the two of them with vivid streaks of orange and pink.

To Cynthia the moment seemed to freeze in time. She felt suspended in a perfect world where desert sunsets were available to anyone with the eyes to seek them out, where love was available in abundance for those who waited for it.

"Do you think we could get you pregnant by Christmas?" Russell whispered mischievously.

"You'd better start to work on that new project right away," she replied.

"Nag, nag, nag," he chided, pulling her arms around his neck so that she could float on his back as he swam to shore. "What would I do without you!"